SABOTAGE!

Lauren Nichols and her sister Jessica are part of a group of friends travelling to Notre-Dame-des-Bois in France for a five-day rally of classic car enthusiasts.

From the start, Lauren is strongly attracted to Rafe Corsini, a newcomer to the gang. But jealousies and rivalries soon flare, and it becomes apparent that someone is targeting members of the group by sabotaging their cars . . .

KATE FINNEMORE

◆

SABOTAGE!

Complete and Unabridged

LINFORD
Leicester

First published in Great Britain in 2020

First Linford Edition
published 2023

A catalogue record for this book is available
from the British Library.

ISBN 978–1–4448–5111–3

Published by
Ulverscroft Limited
Anstey, Leicestershire

Printed and bound in Great Britain by
TJ Books Ltd., Padstow, Cornwall

This book is printed on acid-free paper

New Man On The Scene

'It'll be great,' Lauren Nichols said, glancing at her sister as she steered the car round the roundabout, 'meeting up with all the others again, won't it, Jess?'

'That must be the millionth time you've said that this morning.' There was scorn in Jessica's voice.

'And that must be the millionth time you've checked your phone,' Lauren shot back as the old rivalries flared. But she was at the wheel of her prized 1933 Riley March Special, the wind was in her hair, and they were on their way to a classic car rally in France. She was not going to let herself be put down by her older sister, she decided.

Bumping over the railway tracks, she glanced again at Jessica. Her head was bent, her attention on the phone in her lap. Lauren saw the dejection that made her shoulders slump, and her heart ached for her.

'Jess, stop it.' She reached over and

squeezed the hand that held the phone. 'Stop checking for messages. You're just torturing yourself. You broke it off with him, remember.'

'I know.' Jessica's smile was bleak, and Lauren sighed. Her sister's engagement to Steve Hennessy had brought the two rival family firms, Nichols Classic Cars and Hennessy Motors, together.

But all that had finished two weeks before when the couple split up and Steve had moved to a job hundreds of miles away.

A cousin from France, Raphaël Corsini, was coming to fill the top vacancy at Hennessy Motors. He'd also be joining their group, heading over to France for the rally.

Raphaël. Such an evocative name. But what would the man himself be like?

'Hey,' Lauren said, seeing the sheds, hangars and lines of lorries and cars ahead of her. 'We're there. And what do you know — we're first.'

They'd arrived at the rendezvous, a small parking area a little way inside the ferry terminal precinct. She drew the Riley to a halt. Beside her, Jessica pulled off her 1930s leather pilot's helmet and goggles, shaking her hair free before pushing the car door open. Lauren got out, too, glad to be able to stretch her legs after the hour-long drive.

Several other cars went past them, joining the lines of vehicles waiting to board the ferry before she saw a car she knew well, a lovely old dark green Bentley, coming around the roundabout.

'Steve's car,' Jessica breathed, and there was pain in her voice. Hugging her arms across her chest, she turned and moved away.

Lauren's heart twisted. Poor Jessica. The car belonged to Hennessy Motors, and it had been Steve Hennessy who'd always driven it in the past, with Jessica at his side in the passenger seat.

Steve wasn't behind the wheel today, of course. Lauren watched with interest as the Bentley approached, keen to get her first glimpse of the new man at Hennessy Motors, Raphaël Corsini. She saw

Jessica give him a quick backward glance as she moved away before concentrating yet again on her phone.

He'd driven with the top down, and the wind was ruffling his thick, dark hair. He was in his mid to late twenties, she guessed, her gaze lingering on the strong lines of his face. A shiver of awareness sped down her spine, and there was a tension about her as she watched him pull to a halt a couple of metres from her.

Lauren was still watching — she couldn't take her eyes off him — as he got out of the Bentley and came round the car towards her, walking with an easy, long-legged stride. He was tall and broad-shouldered, and wore jeans and a dark grey T-shirt.

His eyes went from her to her sister, some ten or twelve metres away, and back to her.

'Lauren Nichols.' It wasn't a question. It took just one look at her stunning sister — he'd clearly been told which was which. 'Rafe Corsini.' His voice was deep, attractive, and he had a distinct French accent.

'Not 'Raphaël'?'

'No.' He held out his hand. But he wasn't smiling, and Lauren found herself stiffening. Was there a hint of hostility in his attitude? Or was she being over-sensitive?

Her handshake was brief.

'It's still early in the day. Not yet eight o'clock. The others will be here soon.'

'I look forward to meeting them.'

The emphasis on the word 'them' was very slight, almost imperceptible. But yes, there was a definite edge of hostility in his tone — aimed at her, and almost certainly at her sister, too. With an effort, Lauren brought a smile to her lips.

'There'll be nine of us, on this five-day jaunt in France. You'll find we're a mixed bunch. But I'm certain we'll all do our best to make sure we get on well together.'

An eyebrow went up. His mouth quirked at the corners, and Lauren had the sense he'd taken her words for the warning they were — and, oddly, that he respected her for giving it.

'Of course, mademoiselle.'

His eyes didn't leave hers. For a long moment, the only sound was the shriek of seagulls circling low. Then movement and the sound of car engines coming closer, slowing down, caught her attention.

'Ah, here come some of the others,' she said, hard put to hide the relief in her voice.

There were three cars, travelling in convoy. Lauren knew the first two well, a 1950 Riley Roadster and a 1934 Austin Seven. She waved to their occupants, including the yellow Labrador in the Riley. Behind them came a beautiful midnight-blue Lancia driven by someone she didn't recognise.

'Come and meet them,' she said to Rafe.

She walked, almost ran, over to her friends, leaving him to follow. Hearing the clack of heels on concrete, she looked across to see that Jessica had put her phone away and was joining them.

The Lancia owner on the other hand, a man in his late thirties, she thought, was staying close to his car. Lauren was amused to see him pull a cloth from his pocket, turn his back on her — on them all — and start to polish the mirror-like perfection of his car's bodywork.

Bob Cowley, almost twice Lauren's age, forty-four to her twenty-three, his hair styled in a high, rounded 1950s pompadour Elvis would have been proud of, enveloped her in a bear-hug and she thought no more about it.

'Lauren, love, you look a picture. Jessica, too. A sight for sore eyes. Give us a hug, Jess, love.'

'Let me introduce Rafe Corsini,' Lauren said. 'He's — uh — come to work for his uncle now that Steve has gone up north.'

There were handshakes for Rafe and hugs and kisses for everyone else, apart from the Lancia owner who was still busy with his car.

Everyone was talking at once.

'I've brought cake,' Sarah Osborne said. 'And a couple of quiches,' she added, gesturing toward the cool box behind the passenger seat of the Austin Seven. 'All home-made, that goes without saying.'

'I think I've got a problem with the tappets, Lauren,' Sarah's husband Dave said. 'Could you have a look some time?'

'No problem. You didn't bring little Milo with you?' Lauren asked.

'No. He's spending the weekend with Sarah's mum. We'll pick him up late Monday, when we get back from France.'

'Shame your dad couldn't come on the rally this year,' Bob said to the girls. 'Especially as it's his baby.'

Lauren and Jessica's father owned Nichols Classic Cars. It was he who had organised their first outing the previous year to the classic car rally in the small town of Notre-Dame-des-Bois.

'It's his thyroid,' Lauren replied. 'Overactive. He's got to have a whole load of tests. He thought it best to stay behind.'

'This is Belle,' Bob's wife Brenda, a teacher like her husband, said with a proud smile. Jessica had crouched to make a fuss of the honey-coloured Labrador. The dog rolled on to its back, tail wagging like fury, loving every minute of it. 'She's a rescue dog, but she's as good as gold.'

'She's adorable, Bren,' Jessica said. Getting to her feet, she turned and walked slowly away. Lauren gave an inward sigh.

Her sister's phone was in her hand again.

Other eyes, too, were following her.

'Jessica's already in costume, I see,' Bob said.

'Jessica's always in costume,' Lauren said, not much liking the hint of sharpness that had entered her voice. Her dress-designer sister was wearing one of her own creations. Her version of a car mechanic's overalls was a narrow-cut all-in-one in a soft green that made her tall, slim figure look even taller and slimmer. Lauren, a head shorter than Jessica, was in jeans and a T-shirt. Practical as always, she thought, wishing — not for the first time — that she could be more like her sister.

'Still,' she went on, 'she's made me a beautiful nineteen-thirties dress for the farewell dance on Sunday.'

'You'll be the belle of the ball, Lauren, love,' Brenda said.

'Not me.' Lauren laughed. 'I'll be the one fixing the lights or tinkering with the sound system.'

'So, er, Jessica and Steve . . . ?' Sarah's voice trailed into silence.

Lauren shook her head.

'She thinks it's for the best.' She glanced across at her sister. Once again, her eyes were fixed on the screen of her phone. 'But it's breaking her heart.'

She watched as Jessica went up to the Bentley, and something inside her tightened when Rafe joined her sister. He was speaking to her, and all the while she ran her hands restlessly along the top edge of the passenger-side door.

'Lauren, you must meet Aurélien,' Brenda said. 'Aurélien,' she called to the owner of the Lancia, 'come and say bonjour to Lauren.'

'He's French, too?'

'Yes. He came over last weekend for a gathering of Lancia drivers and spent a few days with us afterwards, and now he's driving back to Notre-Dame-des-Bois with us. It means there'll be ten of us, but that's not a problem, is it?'

Lauren shot Brenda an amused look as the Lancia owner gave the car's immaculate paintwork one final, lingering touch of the polishing cloth before heading over towards them.

He was in his thirties or early forties, she decided, about the same age as Bob. There was an air of old-fashioned Gallic charm about him, and she wondered for an instant if he was going to kiss her hand. When he took it in a brief handshake, with a softly murmured, '*Enchanté, mademoiselle*,' she didn't know whether to be disappointed or not. It would have been a first, after all.

'You have a lovely car,' she said, aware that she felt far more at ease with him than she had with Rafe Corsini.

'A 1925 Lancia Lambda. With the new four-speed gearbox they installed that year.'

'Ah.' And with that, Lauren fell into a happy discussion with him about the improvements Lancia had made to their cars throughout the Twenties.

'You speak very good English,' she said at last.

He shrugged.

'Thank you. I teach English at the senior school in Notre-Dame-des-Bois, and my wife — my ex-wife — is English.'

He stopped, and both he and Lauren looked round as, with a ferocious double de-clutch that made conversation impossible, a 1952 MG swept into the car park and pulled to a halt in a flurry of dust next to the Bentley. The last two members of the group had arrived.

Lauren drew in a steadying breath. She hadn't seen Patrick Henderson since their break-up a week after the rally to

France this time last year. He was the one person she hadn't been looking forward to seeing again.

He jumped out of his MG and came over to the group, a cheerful smile on his face as he shook hands with the men and hugged the women.

Lauren looked past him to his passenger, a woman about her own age who had remained standing beside the car. Like most of the others, she wore the standard uniform of T-shirt and jeans — very skinny jeans.

She was pulling a brush through shoulder-length hair that was a beautiful, deep shade of red. All at once Lauren was aware of her own hair, twisted into an untidy knot at the back of her head.

Patrick stopped in front of her, and she was conscious of that tug of attraction that had made her fall in love with him two years before. There was awkwardness, too.

The silence stretched. She barely heard the chatter of the others around her. Was he going to hug her? Kiss her?

Ignore her?

'Hello, Lauren,' he said.

'Hello, Patrick.' She kept her voice light. 'You're looking well.' Standing on tiptoes, she gave him a little kiss on his cheek. She glanced over his shoulder. His passenger was coming towards him on heels that were even higher than Jessica's. 'Won't you introduce me to your friend?'

He smiled.

'I'll introduce her to everyone.' Stepping back a pace, he reached out a hand, catching the young woman round the waist and drawing her into the group.

'Hey, you all.' He paused, waiting till everyone was listening. Lauren noticed Rafe leave his Bentley and Jessica and head towards the group. 'I'd like you all to meet Chrissie. She's, uh, someone rather special to me.'

The young woman smiled. Her hand sketched a wave.

'Hi.'

'I've drawn up the programme for the weekend's events,' Patrick went on, pulling a folded sheet of paper from the back pocket of his jeans. 'I've got photocopies for you all in the car.

'Lucky I made an extra copy,' he said, glancing across at the Lancia owner. 'We'll go over it on the boat, shall we?'

'He's got it all organised.' It was Rafe, standing beside her. He spoke for her ears only, amusement in his voice, and awareness of his closeness whispered across her skin.

She turned to face him. His eyes were a warm brown, not cold at all, she thought, breathing in an elusive hint of the cologne he wore.

'He's a solicitor,' she murmured. 'He's always had a tendency to take charge.'

Control-freak — that was the word. But she didn't want to be reminded about all that.

'The Bentley's looking good.'

'She is.' If he was surprised by the abrupt change of subject, he didn't show it. 'I've given the engine a complete overhaul, tuned it till she runs like a dream . . .'

They were talking cars, usually a subject of endless fascination as far as Lauren was concerned. This time, though, she found she was listening, but she wasn't taking the words in.

If you could fall in love with the sound of a man's voice, she thought, then she was head over heels. And she loved the way he pronounced her name. Lau-ren. In two distinct syllables. It had never sounded so pretty. So feminine.

All at once it was as if she were in a world of her own, just her and Rafe. The voices of the others seemed to recede to a distant murmur. She was aware of the smile that played over her face, and longed to touch her fingers to his hair, to smooth down the bits that were sticking up.

Suddenly her smile vanished. She frowned.

'What did you say?'

'I said win-at-all-costs rivals Nichols Classic Cars will be battling it out . . .'

'Win at all costs? You're implying my firm uses underhand tactics?' Lauren shook her head in disbelief. 'What put that idea into your head?'

She glanced across at the Bentley. Her sister stood there still, one hand on the bonnet of the car, looking alone and unhappy. The sight brought a tight ache to Lauren's throat.

'Or should I have said 'who'? Jessica?'

Rafe nodded.

'It's not true? Nichols Classic Cars aren't stop-at-nothing rivals?'

'No.'

'Strange. Your sister has more or less admitted it.'

The Same Wavelength?

'Admitted it?' Lauren stared at Rafe.

'Admitted what? I can't imagine what she could have said that would make you think we're playing foul.'

'She never loved Steve.'

'Not true. But anyway, so what?'

'She got him so besotted with her that his work suffered. Hennessy Motors' loss — and Nichols Classic Cars' gain.'

'That's ridiculous.' It was an effort to remain polite. 'I can't believe we're having this conversation. She's been hurt. She wants to hurt someone back. Steve isn't here, so —'

'She told me it was an unexpected bonus when he upped sticks and moved north.'

Frowning, Lauren looked across at her sister and recalled the tears, the growing unhappiness, day on day, week on week, until the day she'd come home to tell them it was all over between her and Steve.

Shaking her head, Lauren looked again into Rafe's unsmiling face. How had she ever thought there was warmth in those eyes?

'Sounds to me,' she said, 'like someone saving face.'

'Maybe you should check with her.'

Lauren's chin came up.

'I don't need to. I know the truth of her relationship with Steve.' She looked around her and forced a smile. 'I think we should rejoin the others, don't you?'

Now that everyone had arrived, it was time to join the line of cars and lorries waiting to board the ferry. But Patrick was insisting on a group selfie first, to record the moment.

'We need to talk,' Lauren murmured to Jessica as they moved towards the others, 'about what you said to Rafe. Not now. When we're back in the car.'

Quickly smoothing loose strands of her hair back into the clasp at the back of her head, she tried to put Rafe Corsini's words, his absurd allegations, out of her mind.

No easy task, she thought, joining the laughing squash as they tried for a group selfie. She could smell the citrus notes of the man's cologne, knew he was standing close by, knew too she was far too aware of him.

'No way we can do a selfie,' Dave said. 'We'll never get all of us in.'

'And what about Belle? She's got to be in the picture, too.'

In the end they asked a lorry driver walking over to his vehicle to take a photo of them all.

'Before we get back into our cars,' Patrick said, holding his arms out to each side to stop anyone moving away. 'I expect we'll all want to do our own thing on the boat. So, shall we say we'll all meet up on deck six at ten-thirty English time, eleven-thirty French time?'

There were murmurs of assent all round, and everyone got into their cars, turning keys, bringing engines back to life, before moving off in a long line.

'I was teasing, all right?' Once again in the Riley's passenger seat, Jessica stared

20

out to her side. There was a sulky edge to her voice.

'Teasing? Well, he's obviously had a humour bypass. He believed every word. He thinks Nichols Classic Cars is out to get Hennessy Motors — by fair means or foul.'

Jessica was silent, still clearly didn't intend turning her head to meet her sister's eyes.

They'd stopped the other side of passport control. Rafe's Bentley was immediately in front of the Riley. Lauren found her gaze skimming his thick, dark hair, his broad shoulders, the arm that was flung out along the back of the passenger seat, and all at once she longed for him to turn round and smile at her.

'You know why Steve and I broke up.'

Jessica had pressed her knuckles to her mouth, and the words came out as an anguished mumble. Lauren blinked back sudden tears for her sister.

'Yes, I know,' she said, swallowing, heart heavy as the line of cars moved off again. 'Things will be OK. You'll see.'

Thirty minutes later, all six cars were parked in one long line on the lowest deck of the ferry. Getting out of her car, Lauren paused an instant to watch Rafe and Aurélien heading for the stairs — although it was Rafe that drew her gaze.

'Will Belle be OK down here?' she asked as Bob and Brenda pulled the soft top up and over their Riley Roadster. Dogs had to stay in their owners' car during the crossing.

'Don't worry, love,' Brenda replied. 'We'll come down halfway through to check up on her. She'll be as right as rain.'

And now Lauren stood alone on the stern deck, forearms resting on the polished wooden rail that ran all round, watching the activity below.

The last of the big lorries were coming on board. The ramps would be going up soon, and they'd be off, heading for France.

She breathed deeply, loving the tang of the salt-laden air, and the warmth of

22

the July sun on her face. She'd pushed that odd, unsettling — what? conversation? confrontation? — with Rafe out of her mind, and excitement, anticipation of a wonderful five-day-long holiday in France, was fizzing through her.

She'd left Jessica and Chrissie in the bar on the other side of the wide stern windows. Her sister had brought out her sketchbook and was showing Chrissie her latest designs.

Patrick was with them, checking something on his tablet. Sarah and Dave had gone down to the cafeteria on the deck below to have a full English breakfast, and the others were scattered around the ship somewhere.

She told herself she didn't want to know where Rafe was, what he was doing — but had to acknowledge it wasn't true.

She pulled her phone out of her pocket and keyed a quick, reassuring text to her parents.

We're on the ferry. Everything's going fine. No breakdowns so far! xx.

Pressing Send and putting her phone back in her pocket, Lauren looked up and her heart skittered into a faster beat. Rafe was coming towards her. She hesitated, not sure whether to keep her expression neutral or to smile a greeting.

'Mind if I join you?' He gestured towards the stern rail.

'Of course not.'

With a mighty creaking and clanking, the first of the ramps started to go up. As one, it seemed, they both turned to lean against the rail, side by side, looking out.

'I love it,' Lauren said, unable to prevent the smile that spread over her face. 'Anything mechanical like this, I just love it.'

She sensed Rafe turn his head to look at her and felt colour warm her cheeks. She'd given herself away. Grease-monkey Lauren, always tinkering with messy car engines. How she wished she could be like Jessica, so feminine — and so confident in her femininity.

'I'm the same,' Rafe said, and she looked at him, surprised — and pleased he hadn't made some condescending remark about her love for all things mechanical.

'Old cars especially,' he went on. 'There's a romance about them that you simply don't get with today's boxes on wheels.'

For a moment she found it difficult to breathe. So he felt it too, that special aura that, for her, had always surrounded old cars. She watched in silence, aware of Rafe's closeness, as the second ramp went up and the ferry pulled away from the dock.

'We're off,' she said.

'Have you been to France before?' Rafe asked a while later.

'Once, that's all. Last year.' Lauren sighed.

So much had changed since then. Last year, she'd been in the MG with Patrick, Jessica in the Bentley with Steve Hennessy, and her parents had taken it in turns to drive the Riley.

'And what did you think of my country, Lauren?'

There it was again, that lovely way he pronounced her name. Lau-ren. She couldn't help smiling.

'I loved it.'

She looked out, remembering, as the ferry moved past the harbour wall to the sea. Seagulls flew low to the water in its wake.

She'd loved the warm, friendly people, the delicious food, the weather, hot and sunny every day. And the hills, the woods and the rambling buildings built of cream-coloured stone in the countryside around Notre-Dame-des-Bois.

'Which part of France do you come from?' she asked. He too had clearly forgotten their conversation or confrontation, call it what you will — or had chosen to put it to one side.

'A small town near Tours. Fairly close to Notre-Dame, in fact. About a hundred kilometres away. Sixty miles,' he added.

'Tell me how Steve happens to have a French cousin.' She turned to look at him and her heart seemed to miss a beat.

He was tall and lean, and the skin of his arms and face glowed with health in the sunlight. The wind was blowing through his hair.

'Sure.' He smiled. 'His father Ted and my mother are brother and sister. She met and married a Frenchman and went to live in France.'

'Your English is very good.'

'My brother, sister and I spent almost every summer holiday here in England with our grandparents.'

They spoke about brothers and sisters, England and France, old cars and new. The thrum of the ship's engine and the constant rush of water as the ferry moved through the sea seemed to exclude everything and everyone else. It was just him and her.

That smile, Lauren knew, was playing over her face again. She had never felt so in tune with anyone before.

'Then your uncle asked you to take over when Steve left,' she said — and instantly regretted it.

'I've got my own business in Tours.'

Rafe clipped the words. 'I'll be heading back there as soon as I get Hennessy Motors back on a — on the correct footing.' He looked out across the water.

The ferry had already travelled quite far into the English Channel. The Sussex Downs were low and smooth in the water, shades of green above the chalk white cliffs.

Lauren sucked in a breath.

'You've got it wrong about Jessica and Steve.'

Rafe twisted to face her, one forearm still leaning on the rail.

'So put me right.'

She shook her head.

'I can't. I'd be betraying a confidence.'

His sound of exasperation only added to her misery. The closeness she'd felt such a short while before might never have been.

'Look,' she said, 'yes, there's rivalry between our two garages, but it's always been friendly.

'OK, the garages are less than thirty miles apart, so it's not ideal. But both draw customers from all over Sussex and beyond. We've got our loyal customer base, and your uncle Ted has got his.'

Lauren looked out to sea and expelled a shaky breath. The sky was blue, hazy along the horizon. Fishing boats and small yachts were dotted here and there on the calm water. So beautiful. But all at once she couldn't bear to look at it any more.

'I'm going inside,' she said, turning away, unable to look at Rafe, unwilling to see the scepticism she just knew was in his eyes.

Jessica was alone. She got to her feet, frowning, when Lauren came in.

'Are you all right?' she asked, putting her arm round her, drawing her to her side.

Lauren scuffed a tear away.

'I'm fine.' She tried for a smile. 'It must be almost time for the ten-thirty meeting.'

'Come on, let's go on down.'

The meeting was on the deck below. The others were already there and had pulled ten of the heavy armchairs into a rough circle. Lauren sat next to Aurélien and watched as, moments later, Rafe came down the stairs, moving with easy, long-legged grace.

Patrick cleared his throat.

'Now we're all here, we can get started. Can you pass these round, please, sweetheart?' He handed Chrissie at his side a small pile of photocopies.

'Everyone got one? OK, so, all being well, we'll arrive in Notre-Dame-des-Bois about seven this evening. We go to our respective B&Bs, freshen up, then we meet our French hosts and have dinner with them at the —'

'*Treille d'Or*,' Aurélien supplied when Patrick hesitated. 'The Golden Vine. The best restaurant in town.'

'Tomorrow there'll be cars arriving from all over France.' Bob Cowley's deep voice rang out as he glanced at his photocopy. 'It'll be a morning for last-minute arrangements, getting everything organised, putting the cars on display in the main square.'

'It was great last year,' Sarah said. 'All those lovely cars. Masses of people turned up.'

'Followed by lunch,' Patrick said, taking charge again. 'And the *concours d'élégance* in the afternoon. The next day, we have the grand parade through the town and out into the countryside.' He paused, drawing a breath.

'Sunday, more of the same, and a farewell dinner and dance in the evening. As usual, there's only one prize on offer, I'm afraid. But it's a big one.'

The news was met with good-natured cheers and jeers. Lauren found herself smiling, leaning forward, taking part. It was good to be back with the group again, although she was uncomfortably aware of Rafe, sitting opposite her. His eyes were on her too often for comfort, she felt.

'We were lucky.' Brenda's voice rose above the others. 'Bill and Mavis won the best of show for us last year. They've got as far as Ankara in Turkey, by the way.'

More cheers. Since their win the previous year, the couple had retired and were touring Europe and Asia in their 1963 Bedford Dormobile.

'And the year before that,' Brenda went on, 'it was someone from a Scottish club.'

'So it'll be a real feather in our cap,' Patrick cut in, 'if a British car can win for the third year running. Any questions?'

The meeting broke up ten or so minutes later. Everyone started to drift away.

'Time for something to eat, sweetheart.'

'How did you get that fantastic shine on the Lancia, Aurélien?'

'Come on, Bob, love. Let's go down and check Belle's OK.'

Soon, only Lauren, Jessica and Sarah remained.

'I must show you the photos of little Milo,' Sarah said, taking her phone out of her handbag. 'He's walking now.'

'Oh!' Jessica jumped up. 'I think I'll catch up with Brenda and Bob, see how Belle's been getting on.'

Sarah looked in surprise at Lauren.

'Is your sister all right?' she asked, once Jessica was out of earshot.

Lauren managed a bright smile.

'She's fine.'

She moved into the armchair next to Sarah's, looked at each photo, made appropriate comments. But her mind was elsewhere, back on the ferry's top deck, watching England disappear from sight, with Rafe at her side.

She was annoyed with herself. She'd over-reacted. That feeling of being on the same wavelength as him, she realised, had existed only in her imagination.

Under Suspicion

'That was quick. We'll be moving out. Any moment.' The ferry had reached Dieppe at two in the afternoon. In no time at all, it seemed, the ramps had come down, and the cars, lorries and caravans could start rolling out on to French soil.

Lauren was at the wheel of her Riley on the bottom deck, Jessica at her side. Fingers fumbling a little, she loosened her hair before re-twisting and fastening it with the clasp to the back of her head.

She turned to look behind her at Bob and Brenda's Riley Roadster. The couple had put the soft top down, and Belle the Labrador, safe in her harness in the back seat, was sitting up, looking round with interest. Lauren turned back to face the front, running her fingertips over the dials on the dash.

'For goodness' sake, stop fidgeting, will you,' Jessica said.

'Yeah, sorry.' Lauren laughed. Anything to avoid looking at Rafe in the car in front.

She saw him reach forward to turn the Bentley's engine on and did the same with the Riley, heaving a mental sigh of relief when the car started first time. Slowly, she followed him out of the ferry.

'Going back to what you said to Rafe, Jess,' she began. She could broach the subject now — the noise of car engines meant there was no risk of being overheard. 'Telling him you'd never been in love with Steve.'

She brought the car to a halt in one of the two lines waiting to go through the passport check and turned to her sister. She wanted to see her face.

Jessica was tucking her hair up into her leather flying helmet. The goggles were for show only. She never pulled them down over her eyes.

'Give it a rest, can't you? We don't have to talk about it now.'

'Yes. We do.' Lauren edged the car forward a few metres as the vehicles in front moved on. 'Saying you made him so crazy about you, he couldn't concentrate on work. Saying you deliberately drove Steve away, knowing his firm would suffer. What was that all about?'

In the middle of buckling the strap under her chin, Jessica paused and looked at her sister.

'I couldn't tell him the real reason.'

Lauren drew in a breath.

'No, I suppose not,' she conceded. 'But Rafe is convinced Nichols Classic Cars is out to ruin Hennessy Motors. The two garages are deadly rivals.' She looked over at him, at the back of his head, his dark hair, in his Bentley in the other line of cars. Time after time her eyes were drawn to him. 'But we're not rivals. Not really.'

'Yes, we are. Of course we are. Both garages buy, fix and sell classic cars as well as all the modern stuff. Of course they're in competition. Don't be such an idiot.'

Lauren bit back a retort. Jessica was talking not to her but at her, just as she had so often in the past, with all the contempt of an older sister for her younger sibling. It hurt, just as it always had.

'You're so naïve, Lauren.' Jessica clearly hadn't finished. 'You know nothing about business.'

'And you do of course,' she retorted, stung.

'You should stick to messing about with engines.'

'And maybe you should think about telling Rafe the truth.'

The two sisters fell silent. Lauren waited in the line, moving the car forward a few metres at a time, Jessica's sharp words an angry echo in her mind.

Yes, she 'messed about with engines', working in her father's garage. But she was doing well. Only that year she'd been put in charge of the Classic Car repair department. She couldn't match her sister for ambition, though.

Jessica had started with a small shop/workshop in one of the cheaper parts of Brighton, designing and making clothes, specialising in evening and wedding dresses. She was still in the same shop but had built up an ever-growing clientele and a flourishing website.

Lauren sighed. She'd always felt she was in the shadow of her beautiful, talented, creative older sister. They were like chalk and cheese. Oil-smeared overalls against effortless elegance.

With a start she saw they'd reached the checkpoint. Jessica handed over their passports with a smile and a confident '*Bonjour, monsieur*' that were in total contrast to the way she'd spoken to her sister only minutes before. Tears came to Lauren's eyes. Blinking, she turned her head away and told herself to put the nasty little spat out of her mind.

Aurélien's midnight-blue Lancia, boxier in shape than the later cars, had already gone through and was waiting, as arranged, in the car park on the other side of the checkpoint.

Rafe's car in Bentley racing green, and Bob's orange-red Roadster joined him even as she watched, followed by Patrick and Chrissie and Sarah and Dave.

'OK. Double-check, everyone,' Patrick called out as Lauren and Jessica drove into the car park, pulling the Riley up alongside Rafe's Bentley. 'Each driver has got the phone numbers of the other drivers, yes?'

Lauren patted the phone in the back pocket of her jeans, glanced across at Rafe and saw him nod.

'Yes,' she called back, one voice among many. They'd start off as a convoy, she knew. But with faster, more modern cars overtaking first one, then another, it wouldn't stay that way. If anything happened, they would phone the others.

And with shouts of 'Have a good journey', all six cars were moving off, round the roundabout and up the hill that took them along the outskirts of Dieppe, heading south towards Rouen and beyond. They were on their way.

The convoy of cars left the fast dual carriageway as soon as they could, taking the old main road south. The afternoon air was warm and sweet with the scent of wildflowers and grass, and salt from the sea. The sky was a magnificent cloudless blue.

Lauren's Riley March Special was going like a dream. She started humming a song. On the open road, with the wind tugging softly at her hair, she could almost forget her heated exchange with her sister — and the conflicting emotions Rafe Corsini aroused in her.

All at once, Jessica turned in her seat, reaching a hand out to Lauren, her touch light as her fingers brushed strands of her sister's hair back from her face.

'I'm sorry, Lauren.' She bent her head close to her sister's to be heard above the noise of the engine and the wind rushing past. 'I don't know what got into me. It's seeing the Bentley. Missing Steve . . .'

Jessica's voice trailed away. She shook her head, sat back in her seat, looked down at her hands twisting in her lap, and Lauren felt that familiar tightness in her chest as she shared her sister's pain.

Her phone was vibrating. With a frown she pulled it out of the back pocket of her jeans and handed it to Jessica.

'Can you take it?' They'd barely covered 15 miles. Too soon for someone to suggest stopping for coffee. It had to be bad news.

'Hi, Dave. What's up?'

Lauren could see Aurélien's Lancia a long way ahead. Bob and Brenda's Roadster was out of sight. A lorry filled her rear-view mirror, blocking her view of the cars behind.

'The Bentley? Is Rafe OK?'

Lauren's hands tightened on the steering wheel. She glanced at her sister. Jessica nodded reassurance at her, though her expression remained serious, and Lauren's hands relaxed their grip a fraction.

'Good. That's the main thing,' Jessica was saying. 'We'll turn back straight away. Where are you?'

Lauren didn't wait to hear the rest. She pulled in to the side of the road, letting the lorry roar past, did a U-turn and headed back the way they'd come.

'Something to do with the radiator,' Jessica said.

41

They found the others in an off-road picnic area about two miles up the road. Patrick and Chrissie, Dave and Sarah stood in a group round the front end of the Bentley. Rafe lay on the ground on his back. Only his torso and legs were visible. Head, shoulders and arms were under the car.

Lauren pulled to a halt beside the MG, jumped out and ran past the Austin Seven to the Bentley, Jessica close at her heels.

There was a thin, irregular trail of water, dark on the dun-coloured gravel. The Bentley's engine smelled of steam.

Lauren held the flat of her hand close to the radiator and could feel the heat coming off it.

'I don't understand,' Chrissie said, tugging a brush through her hair.

'Well, sweetheart,' Patrick said, 'the temperature gauge told Rafe the engine was getting too hot. That's why he pulled in here.' There was a hint of condescension in the way he spoke, and Lauren winced. That tone had been all too familiar. She'd hoped never to hear it again.

'The radiator was fine this morning.' Rafe's voice, muffled, came from under the car. 'I checked the water level before setting out. Checked everything, in fact.'

'So he knows there must be a leak,' Lauren said.

'And I've found it. Just a minute.'

Seconds later, Rafe wriggled out from under the car and got to his feet, wiping his hands on the cloth he held.

'It wasn't a leak.' His face was set, his eyes had lost all warmth. 'Someone's given the radiator drain tap an eighth of a turn. The water's been draining out, drip by drip, from the moment we left the ferry.'

No-one spoke. Unease whispered across Lauren's skin. It was Sarah who voiced the question uppermost in her mind.

'Someone? Someone from the garage, you mean? By accident?'

'No.' Rafe shook his head. 'I was the one who worked on this car. I don't make mistakes like that. It wasn't an accident.'

He paused and looked at each of them in turn. His gaze came to rest on Lauren.

'It was an act of deliberate sabotage. Someone's trying to put me out of the rally.'

There was a moment's shocked silence.

'Don't be silly, Rafe,' Jessica said. 'Who'd do a thing like that?'

'Whoever did it,' Rafe went on, 'must have done so while we were on the ferry.'

'But you're not allowed down on the car decks during the crossing,' Dave said.

You are if you need to check up on your dog, Lauren thought, turning and moving away. Or if you go down with the people who are checking up on their dog.

She felt sick, troubled by a suspicion that simply couldn't be true, and hugged her arms across her chest. Despite the warmth of the summer afternoon, she shivered.

Jessica had gone down to the car decks

to check on Belle — or that was what she'd said. She'd more or less told Rafe that their father's garage was out to ruin Hennessy Motors. And her break-up with Steve had made her deeply unhappy.

There was another thing — the way Jessica had spoken to Rafe only seconds before. Lauren stopped, turned to look across at her sister and drew in a shaky breath. Had Jessica been just a shade too quick in her reaction? Could it be guilt that had made her snap at him?

One thing was clear: she had to speak to her sister.

Irreconcilable Differences

Rafe stood in the centre of the group, half a head taller than the other two men there, and plainly in control. Lauren saw him say something to Patrick who took his phone out of his pocket. Phoning Aurélien in the Lancia and Bob and Brenda in their Roadster, she imagined, telling them what had happened and giving them directions to the off-road picnic area.

Used to giving orders rather than receiving them, her ex was looking rather put out, she thought, and would have been amused if the whole situation hadn't been so serious.

As so often recently, it seemed, Jessica was standing a little apart from the rest. When she reached her, Lauren touched a finger to her lips, urging her to silence. Hooking an arm round her sister's, she drew her away.

She waited until they were several metres distant from the others, and out of earshot.

'Reassure me please that you had nothing to do with what's happened.' Lauren gestured towards Rafe's car.

'You're joking. Do I really have to answer that?' Both look and tone were scathing.

'Jess. Tell me.'

'Some sister you are. How about some family loyalty here?'

Lauren felt herself flush.

'After everything you told him,' she persisted, 'Rafe's going to be convinced you did it.'

'Well, I didn't.'

'You didn't turn the radiator drain tap?'

'I wouldn't even know where the wretched thing was. Besides, do you seriously think I'd risk getting oil or whatever on this?' She made an up and down movement with both hands, indicating the clothes she wore, her ultra-chic take on a car mechanic's overalls.

A moment to absorb the words. Then Lauren found she was smiling, a smile broad with relief.

'That's a very convincing argument!' The notion that Jessica would ever get under a car to tinker with its engine was too ridiculous for words.

'Though I don't know,' she went on, pretending to consider. 'You could have spread a blanket on the floor, protected your outfit that way.'

'Thanks a bunch.' But Jessica was smiling, and the two sisters met in a heartfelt hug.

'I'm going to have a word with Rafe,' Lauren said, easing away.

'No. It should be me.'

Lauren shook her head.

'He might need practical help, too, getting his car up and running. I'll go.'

'If you insist.'

Rafe watched her approach. His expression could only be described as carefully neutral, she thought, heart pitterpattering an uneasy beat.

'I know what you're thinking, Rafe. Might be thinking,' she corrected. She spoke for his ears alone.

Crowded by the cars and the others in the group, she found herself very close to him, less than a metre away. 'It wasn't Jessica, though. It really wasn't.'

'I'd like to believe that, Lauren.' He, too, spoke softly, and the way he said her name cast its usual spell. 'I really would.' He brought his hand up, palm lightly skimming, once, twice, up and down her arm.

Lauren stilled. The skin of her arm was tingling. But he'd touched her. That was all. So why was she suddenly so breathless?

'Then do believe it. Because it's the truth,' she said, rather more sharply than she'd have wished, and felt colour wash over her face.

The beep of a car horn cut through the air, and she twisted round, welcoming the interruption. Aurélien in his Lancia, and Bob, Brenda and Belle in their Roadster were turning into the picnic area.

'Lucky you spotted something was wrong,' Aurélien said when Rafe had finished explaining to the newcomers what had happened.

'I could smell it. The engine was over-heating.' Rafe's tone was grim. 'If I'd carried on, the whole thing would have seized solid.

'Tell me, Bob,' he continued. 'You went down to the car decks during the crossing to check up on Belle —'

'That's right. Me, Brenda and Jessica.'

Lauren saw Rafe's eyes widen a fraction at mention of her sister's name.

'Did you see anyone else down there?' he asked.

Bob pushed his fingers through his Elvis-style pompadour, shaking his head.

'Sorry. No.'

'People can't go wandering down to the car decks, Rafe love, whenever they feel like it,' Brenda said.

'You can only go down once during the crossing to check on your pet. Plus, a member of the crew has to go down there with you.'

'So it seems likely your imaginings about sabotage, Rafe, are just that —

wild imaginings,' Patrick said.

Rafe sent him a cold look.

'Yeah, maybe I was mistaken and the radiator drain tap simply worked itself loose. Let's get this show back on the road, shall we?'

'Has the engine cooled down enough?' Lauren said.

'My dear sister, always so practical.' Jessica's whisper in her ear made Lauren jump. She hadn't realised she had rejoined the group.

'Here, have a slice of cake, everyone,' Sarah said, clearly forcing good cheer into her voice. She eased the lid off a large tin. 'Lemon drizzle.'

And so, as they waited for the Bentley's motor to cool down, they tucked into homemade cake and ginger beer. Almost as if they had each made a conscious decision, they chatted about everything except what had happened to Rafe's car.

Something close to a party atmosphere developed — though the suspicion of sabotage, inevitably, perhaps, remained a shadow hanging over them.

Aurélien phoned the rally organisers to say they wouldn't make their expected arrival time of seven in the evening. Putting his phone back in his pocket, he addressed the group.

'They assure me,' he said in his precise way, 'that it will be no trouble, no trouble at all, to delay the meal the Treille d'Or is preparing for you.' He smiled. 'They wish us *bonne route*.'

'Uneventful route, I hope,' Dave quipped. 'How do you say that in French?'

'You'll join us for that meal, won't you, Aurélien, love?'

'Oh. I, er —'

'Of course you will. You're one of us now.'

A little over an hour later, the Bentley's radiator had cooled down sufficiently to be topped up with water and the six cars moved off once again in convoy.

Rafe's Bentley was in front, leading the way, with Lauren's Riley next in line and Dave and Sarah's Austin Tourer after that. Whenever the road curved, or they went round a roundabout, Lauren was able to check that the remaining three cars were still following.

So far, so good, she thought, touching the walnut dashboard for luck. Her gaze went to the Bentley in front, taking in Rafe's broad back, and the way the wind was ruffling his dark hair, and her chest grew tight with emotions she was hard pressed to name.

Such an attractive man. Yet he thought someone was intent on putting him out of the rally — and she and her sister were the main suspects.

But it didn't make sense. None of it made sense. Yes, she and Jessica had a motive, she could just about accept that — destroying or seriously damaging a rival's valuable car, or his reputation, or both. It wasn't true, though.

Could it have been sheer chance that the radiator drainage tap worked itself loose? Unlikely, Lauren decided. Rafe had said he'd checked everything, including the radiator. But what if he wasn't as efficient or as thorough as he thought he was?

All at once she pictured his hands on the steering wheel of his car. Strong, competent hands, she thought, recalling with a shiver the way he'd run his hand up and down her arm.

Expelling a shaky breath, she glanced at Jessica and shook her head. Yet again, her sister had her phone on her lap. Waiting — hoping? — for a message from Steve.

'Oh, Jess.' Lauren reached over and squeezed Jessica's forearm. 'Why don't you call him?'

'There's no point.'

'You broke it off, remember. So maybe it's up to you, not him, to make the first move.'

Jessica sent her sister a look full of bitter pain.

'I said there's no point. We'll never agree. 'Irreconcilable differences'. Isn't that what they call it?' She thrust her phone into her bag. 'It's over between us. Full stop.'

They fell silent, the only sounds the

steady rumble of the car engine and the hum of the tyres over tarmac. Then Jessica gestured towards Rafe, some 20 metres ahead.

'He looks good in Steve's car, doesn't he?'

'It's the firm's car, not Steve's.'

'He still looks good in it.' There was an edge Lauren couldn't fathom to her sister's voice. 'In fact,' Jessica went on, 'he's rather dishy, isn't he?'

Lauren tensed. What was her sister getting at? Did she sense the attraction that drew Lauren towards the Frenchman? And, if so, would Jessica tease, or would she sneer?

Lauren forced herself to give a bright, care-free laugh.

'Dishy, yes. And unattached. Up for grabs, even,' she added, making her tone as light as it could be.

* * *

Dave got the uneventful journey he'd wished for. There were no further delays, and they made good time. Even so, it was nine in the evening when the six cars pulled into the main square of Notre-Dame-des-Bois, parking parallel to a beautiful, very old Hispano-Suiza and two iconic Seat 600s. A contingent from Spain, it seemed, would be taking part in the rally.

The square was in fact a rectangle, dotted all over with pompom-shaped lime trees that would provide welcome shade during the heat of the day.

A raised bandstand that wouldn't have been out of place in a British sea-side resort stood in the centre.

Three of the rally organisers were there to greet them and show them to their B&Bs.

'They had intended eating with us,' Rafe said, translating what one of them was telling him. 'But it's so late, they've eaten already.'

'The Treille d'Or's over by the church.' With a quick, cold glare at Rafe, Patrick pointed to his left. 'We'll all meet there at nine-thirty, OK?'

Murmuring their assent as they pulled their luggage out from the back seat of the car, Lauren and Jessica followed one of the organisers through tall, wide double doors into a small courtyard. Lauren hid her surprise when Rafe joined them.

'We stayed here last year,' she said, smiling her delight when the owner of the B&B came out to shake their hands.

The year before, her husband Pierre had been restoring a fabulous 1902 Panhard and Levassor. Was the project still ongoing, she wondered.

'The building dates from the seventeenth century, the time of Richelieu and the Three Musketeers,' Rafe said, translating what Madame Lepage was saying.

The two sisters were sharing a room on the first floor. Lauren looked around her as she walked in, smiling as she took in the high ceiling criss-crossed by dark oak beams, the tall windows and the cool tiled floor.

Jessica bounced on one of the twin beds.

'Seems nice and comfy.' She, too, was smiling.

It was still light, and Lauren moved over to the windows. Looking out across the square, she saw Bob and Brenda had driven their car round to the far side and were about to enter a building over there. Belle was running this way and that, tail wagging like mad.

Dave and Patrick's vehicles were nowhere to be seen. Only the Riley and the Bentley remained, parked side by side next to the Spanish cars in the square below. Aurélien must have taken his Lancia, heading home to freshen up before the evening meal.

With a contented sigh, Lauren crossed to the en-suite and pulled open the door. 'Who's first for the shower?'

'You go first. I'm going to unpack.'

Fifteen minutes later, Lauren was towelling her hair dry and looking with some apprehension at the dress Jessica had laid out on the bed for her. Her sister had designed and made it specially for her, she knew. Bias-cut from a silky rayon crepe in a deep plum colour that went perfectly with her pale skin, it was soft and feminine. Too feminine? Lauren was at her happiest when dressed in jeans and T-shirt.

'Go on, put it on,' Jessica said, coming out of the bathroom.

'I don't usually —'

'I know. I've got trousers lined up for you for tomorrow night. Wide-legged, high-waisted sailor's trousers. You'll love them.' Jessica spoke with enthusiasm. 'You're driving a nineteen-thirties car so you've got to wear nineteen-thirties clothes. Simples. Put it on, go on.'

With a laugh, Lauren did so, slipping the dress on over her head and pulling the side zip up. She'd leave her hair loose, she decided.

'Which room do you think Rafe's in?' Jessica asked, stepping into sea-blue lounge pyjamas — another of her own designs. When they'd reached the first-floor landing of the B&B, the sisters had gone in one direction and Rafe in the other.

'This place is only small,' Lauren said. 'Maybe he's in the one I had last year.' And it was somehow disconcerting to imagine him where she'd been the year before, in the room that looked out on to an orchard of plum and apricot trees, the brightly coloured fruit ripening in the hot July sun.

'Do a twirl,' Jessica ordered. 'You look lovely, Lauren. You really do.'

'So do you.' With the fabric of her lounge pyjamas floating and flowing around her, her sister looked simply stunning.

'Let's knock 'em for six, doll,' Jessica said in her hammiest Hollywood accent.

Laughing, they left their room, ran down the stairs and let themselves out through the front door — to find Rafe waiting for them in the courtyard.

In dark shirt and trousers that emphasised his height and the lean strength of his body, he too looked stunning. But it was the smile that curved his mouth as he looked up from his phone and watched the sisters draw near that made the breath catch in Lauren's throat.

Evidently he'd decided to call a truce — and that was fine with her.

'A shower and a change of clothes have done you the power of good,' she said with an answering smile.

'And you both look wonderful. But —' He looked at his phone with exaggerated emphasis. 'It's nine twenty-seven precisely. Control-freak Patrick will be fretting. Shall we go?'

Lauren smiled again, a wry inward smile this time. It hadn't taken Rafe long to size Patrick up. If only she'd been as quick to realise what he was like.

'Permit me, mesdemoiselles.' Rafe linked arms with both Lauren and Jessica, drawing the two sisters to his sides. As if it was the most natural thing in the world, Lauren thought, far too aware of the warmth of his body so close to hers as they walked three abreast, crossing the square to the Treille d'Or.

Swifts wheeled high in the sky. The skirts of Lauren's dress swayed as she walked, brushing against her bare legs.

The evening air was warm and still, and full of enticing scents. She took deep breaths and listened, every sense alive, as Rafe told them a story he'd learned about the restaurant.

Halfway across, they were joined by Sarah and Dave, moments later by Bob and Brenda with Belle on a lead.

'You look beautiful, Lauren. Good enough to eat. Doesn't she, Bren, love? And what about you, Jess — a sight for sore eyes.'

Just as they reached the restaurant, the midnight blue Lancia purred to a halt beside them and Aurélien jumped out.

'I am not late, I hope.'

A waiter led the eight of them through the restaurant and out into a garden at the rear. Chrissie and Patrick were already there, sitting opposite each other at one end of a long table set for ten.

Patrick looked pointedly at his phone before laying it on the table. Unable to prevent a smile, Lauren turned round, her glance finding Rafe a short way behind her.

With an ironic lift of his eyebrows he smiled back, and Lauren had to look down, surprised by the warmth of the feelings that brief, shared instant had aroused in her.

Recurring Dream

Sitting down at the other end of the table from Patrick, Lauren found she was next to Aurélien. Rafe was opposite her, and Jessica diagonally opposite. A waiter served tall, narrow glasses of a pale gold liquid tinged with a blush of pink.

'Kir, Lau-ren. Local bubbly with —' Rafe brought his glass to his nose '– a dash of raspberry liqueur. We'll start the meal by wishing each other *santé* — good health.'

Lauren was smiling. She couldn't help it. She was sitting opposite Rafe, had the perfect excuse for her gaze to linger over his features. She could see each curling eyelash, the shadow of next day's beard along the strong lines of his jaw, the thick dark hair she longed to run her fingers through. And of course, she could listen to her heart's content to his beautiful voice.

'Everyone's been served, Rafe,' Jessica prompted, and with a smile he chinked glasses with her, then with Lauren and Aurélien.

'*Santé.*'

Scraping back their chairs, he and his fellow countryman stood up, wishing good health to all the others round the table. Laughing, everyone followed suit, chinking glasses before taking their first sips of their drinks.

Fine streams of tiny bubbles in Lauren's glass were shooting to the surface, catching at her nostrils as she sipped.

'Let's toast, too,' she said, speaking to the whole group, 'to an enjoyable few days — for us and for our cars — here in this lovely part of France.'

There was laughter, and murmurs of 'Hear, hear' and 'Let's hope . . . no more incidents.' Belle, lying on her side behind Brenda's chair, raised her head and gave a single bark.

'Belle agrees, Lauren, love,' Bob said as they all sat back down again.

Everyone was chatting at once, enjoying their kirs, the lingering warmth of the summer evening and the tantalising savoury smells that drifted on the still air from the restaurant's kitchens.

Making some smiling remark to Sarah who was sitting the other side of Aurélien, Lauren turned back to face Rafe — and all at once it was as if a breath of chill wind was whispering along the skin of her arms. He and her sister were deep in conversation, heads turned towards each other, leaning close, as though they were the only two people in the world.

For one crazy moment she even wished Jessica had her phone out instead, staring at its screen, hoping against hope for a message from Steve.

But she heard Jessica laugh, saw her manicured fingers reach out to touch Rafe's wrist, and her mind flashed back to the moment as they entered the restaurant when Patrick had looked at his phone, wordlessly telling them all they were late, and Rafe's eyes had met hers.

She swallowed. That brief moment of shared amusement, shared intimacy, might never have happened, she thought sadly.

Bringing a smile to her face, she looked at Aurélien.

'Is this place new? It looks it. We didn't come here last year, that I do know,' she said, aware her tone was a shade too bright.

He ran his fingers along the thin line of his moustache. He reminded her of a 1920s film star.

'You were here last year, in Notre-Dame-des-Bois?'

'Yes, don't you remember? A couple from our group won best of show.' She saw his mouth tighten a fraction. 'Oh, you weren't here, I take it.'

'I was in the UK, spending the summer holidays with my wife and son, and my wife's family.'

'Ah.'

The starter, a tartare of fresh and smoked salmon, was brought out, outside lights were turned on, and tall lighted candles were placed on the table.

Slanting a glance at Rafe and Jessica, Lauren thought she heard the words 'Hennessy Motors'. The two of them were still deep in a conversation that seemed to exclude all others.

But there was a seriousness, an earnestness, about them that she hadn't seen before. Was it possible they were talking business, she wondered — and the relief that washed through her took her by complete surprise.

'Bon appétit,' she said to the table in general and took a piece of crusty bread from the basket Dave was holding out. 'Notre-Dame-des-Bois is a really nice town, isn't it?' she said to Aurélien.

Yet again, his mouth tightened.

'My wife — my ex-wife — did not like it much. Too small. Too rural. The people too provincial in their attitudes.'

'Oh.' Lauren didn't know what to say. The divorce — and the bitterness — were clearly far too recent, too raw.

'Our house — my house — is in a tiny hamlet some eight kilometres away. For her it was the back of beyond. Anyway,' he went on, dabbing his serviette to his moustache, 'we are divorced now. That is one episode of my life that is over. She and our son are back in Manchester.'

'Will you get to see him?'

He smiled.

'Yes. School holidays. Now, let me pour you some wine. Hmm, a pinot noir, a full-bodied white, perfect with salmon,' he said with a return of the old-fashioned charm that had struck her the first time she'd met him, on the parking area in Newhaven.

'Tell me about restoring the Lancia,' she invited. 'Where did you find her, to start with?'

'Yes,' Dave said from further along the table. 'Where did you source the spare parts?'

Fascinated as always by any talk of cars, Lauren ate her salmon tartare, sipped the delicious wine and joined in the discussion with enthusiasm. And only occasionally did she look at her sister and Rafe, still deep in their own discussion.

But when the main course, fillet of beef with fennel and sautéed new potatoes, was served, Rafe was leaning back

in his chair, the hint of a frown across his forehead, narrowed eyes on Jessica. Going over in his mind what she'd told him?

'Another first-class local wine. We always drink a red with beef, of course,' Aurélien said, filling the glasses of those around him. Dave passed the bread basket along.

'The food's delicious,' Lauren said, cutting into her fillet, breathing in the rich, meaty aroma. 'Good thing none of us is vegetarian.'

'I am,' Chrissie said from the far end of the table. 'Well, almost. Pescatarian. I sometimes eat fish.'

Patrick reached across the table to cover his girlfriend's hand with his.

'But I've persuaded her to eat normally while we're here.'

'Persuaded her?' Lauren's voice was cold.

She sensed Rafe sit up straight and darted a glance at him. He was looking at Patrick, unsmiling, shoulders taut.

Leaning forward, she saw Chrissie had

pushed the meat to one side of her plate.

'You should have mentioned it to the organisers, Patrick, before we came over.'

'Uh, I expressed myself badly. What I meant to —'

'The restaurant would have provided a vegetarian meal if they'd known,' Rafe cut in, his tone grim. Raising a hand, he brought a waiter running and spoke in rapid French. Belle growled, picking up on the tension perhaps. The waiter hastened back inside, sweeping Chrissie's plate up as he went.

For a long moment no-one spoke. Rafe and Patrick, at opposite ends of the table, held each other's gaze.

'An oversight on my part. A regrettable oversight.' Mouth pursed, Patrick bit each word out. Turning to his girlfriend, he said, 'Forgive me, sweetheart?'

Chrissie must have nodded — Lauren had leaned back and could no longer see her from where she was sitting — and everyone else started talking again, bringing wine glasses to lips, tucking into the main course with great relish.

'Lasagnes d'aubergine.' With a flourish, the waiter set a plate on the table in front of Chrissie.

Rafe leaned towards Lauren.

'You did the right thing, calling him out on that.'

'His choice of words just got to me,' she said, conscious of the warm glow Rafe's praise had sent flowing through her.

The cheese course — grilled goats' cheese on small rounds of toasted bread, served with a salad — was followed by dessert, a rum baba with strawberries and cream.

Along with everyone else, Lauren chatted, laughed and joked. It was an evening that would remain in her memory for a long time. The company, the delicious food and wine, the ambience — in the garden of a restaurant in France on a warm summer's evening — all contributed to make it a meal she wouldn't forget.

But there were other reasons too,

tensions that bubbled close to the surface: the growing dislike Rafe and Patrick plainly felt for each other, Aurélien's bitterness towards his British ex-wife and above all, the mystery of the leak from the Bentley's radiator.

Rafe had spoken no more about it. Did he still think it was a deliberate act of vandalism? Sabotage? Did he still think she or Jessica was responsible?

She sighed. The year before, it had all been quite different. Then, her parents had been with them, an older, calming influence.

Jessica and Steve had been completely wrapped up in each other, to the exclusion of all else. And she, Lauren, had been with Patrick — and coming to the realisation that their relationship was drawing to its end.

'It's gone eleven, folks.' Brenda's voice broke into her thoughts. 'Time to call it a day. Up early tomorrow morning.'

With mock groans all round, everyone drained their glasses, pushed their chairs back, and made their way outside to the square. Soft calls of 'Goodnight' and 'Sleep well' hovered in the air as they drifted away in twos and threes, heading for their B&Bs, or, in Aurélien's case, his midnight-blue Lancia.

With a farewell wave as the Lancia went on its way, Rafe linked arms once again with Lauren and Jessica, and they headed towards Madame Lepage's house.

'Were you jealous?' Jessica asked moments later, stepping out of her lounge pyjamas. 'Because Rafe was monopolising me?'

'Jealous? No, of course not.' Afraid her features might tell a different tale, Lauren took far longer than she normally would to pull her dress up over her head.

'Bet you were really.'

'Jess, stop it. You're teasing, and I don't like it.'

'Will Rafe be dreaming of you tonight? Or me?'

'Jessica,' Lauren warned. For of course she was jealous — and didn't like herself for it.

'You or me?' Jessica challenged, picking up the square, French-style pillow from her bed and holding it up, ready to throw.

With a laugh Lauren snatched her own pillow up.

'Neither of us, you idiot. For all we know, there's someone else in his life already.'

'There isn't.'

'No?' Lauren lowered her pillow. From outside, through the open window, came the hoot of an owl. Hard to believe they were in the middle of a town. Though, going by the number of inhabitants, by British standards it was more a village than a town.

'He told you that?'

Her sister nodded.

'The two of you were getting on like a house on fire.' Lauren hoped her sister wouldn't hear the sharp, unhappy edge of accusation in her voice.

Letting her pillow drop, Jessica pulled her sister into a hug.

'I'm sorry I teased you. Listen —'
Pushing Lauren gently away, she took
her pillow and threw it on the bed before
clasping her forearms. 'It wasn't what
you think. I wasn't making a play for
him. We were talking about Hennessy
Motors.'

Lauren bit her lip. Her sister looked
desperate to convince. And what she
was saying had the ring of truth.

Frowning, Jessica continued.

'Rafe wasn't giving much away but
I got the impression the business isn't
doing too well.'

Lauren frowned, too.

'Good news for Dad, I suppose.'
But bad news for Rafe. A rival going
under — the thought should have
delighted her. Instead — because it was
Rafe? — it made her unbearably sad.

* * *

'Are you sure I can't help?' Jessica asked.

Lauren laughed. It was the next morning and the two of them were getting

ready to go down for breakfast. Her sister had spent over half an hour doing her hair, her makeup and her nails.

Still in 1930s mode, she'd put on a neat, feminine blouse and long, wide trousers pleated at the front, finishing the outfit with heels that had to be higher than those Chrissie had worn the evening before. She had her phone out, fingers moving fast over the screen.

Lauren, on the other hand, had twisted her hair into a knot fastened by a clasp and put on her usual uniform of jeans, T-shirt and trainers.

It was a practical choice. She'd be working on her car that morning and possibly helping others with theirs so, even though she'd be pulling overalls on over the top, it made sense to keep her hair off her face and wear old, sensible clothes.

'I suppose you could always flick a feather duster round the Riley's upholstery. Prettily, of course.'

Jessica pulled a face.

'Thanks a bunch. You got up early,'

she went on, looking up from her phone. 'I heard you opening the shutters. Restless night?'

'A bit,' Lauren said, and felt colour wash up through her cheeks.

The understatement of the century, she thought, turning away so that her sister couldn't see her face. It had been one of those dreams that recurred, over and over throughout the night — walking across the square with Rafe, side by side, arms linked, and he'd stopped, swinging her round to face him, drawing her close, gathering her into a kiss that went on and on . . .

'I watched the goings-on out there in the square. Very interesting,' she said, and it was an effort to put conviction into her voice. 'A council truck watering the hanging baskets. Another emptying the bins. I saw a fox, too.'

For some reason, she didn't tell her sister she'd also seen Rafe. When he emerged out of the B&B dressed for jogging in T-shirt and shorts, she'd stepped back from the window just enough not to be seen if he'd looked up. She'd watched his tall, lean figure as he ran along the road that skirted the square before disappearing down one of the side streets.

'Fascinating.' Jessica's tone was dry. 'Shall we go down?' she said, putting her phone back in her pocket and opening the door to their room. The aroma of fresh-brewed coffee wafted up from below.

They met Rafe at the top of the stairs, coming from his own room along the other corridor. His thick dark hair, still damp from the shower, stuck up in unruly spikes, and the breath caught in Lauren's throat.

'Snap,' he said with a smile, gesturing towards the clothes she wore. He'd changed and was now wearing jeans and trainers, and a faded red T-shirt that had seen better days.

'*Bonjour*, Lauren,' he murmured, and to her surprise he leaned down to give her a kiss on each cheek. 'Did you sleep well?'

'Um, very well.' She could still feel the light rasp of his jaw against the skin of her face, smell the citrus notes of his soap, long moments after he'd turned to greet her sister in the same way, and wondered at the smile that curved his lips. He surely couldn't even suspect how she'd dreamed of him during the night. Could he?

In the dining-room, they sat down round three sides of a rectangular table, with Jessica on Lauren's left and Rafe opposite.

Madame Lepage brought in coffee, milk and sugar cubes, followed by a basket of flaky croissants and pains au chocolat and another of fresh, crusty bread, pointed out the two types of jam and the butter, and left them to enjoy their breakfasts.

'So, *mesdemoiselles*,' Rafe said, pouring coffee for the three of them, 'what are your plans for this morning?'

'Well, I messaged Chrissie, asking if she'd like to explore the town with me.' As Jessica spoke, her phone pinged. Her face lit up as she looked at the screen. 'She would. Great.'

'What about you, Lauren?'

'I promised Dave I'd have a look at his Austin. And I must make sure the Riley is in tip-top shape for the rally.'

'Mind if I tag along?'

Breaking open a length of bread, Lauren looked up sharply, unable to imagine Rafe just 'tagging along' anywhere. She slanted a sideways glance at her sister. But Jessica was sipping her coffee, busy on her phone and paying no heed to the conversation.

'Don't you need to check over the Bentley?'

He smiled.

'Plenty of time for that.'

Lauren stiffened. Was there something a shade too casual about his tone, his manner? The very French way he'd greeted her that morning, her dream-plagued night, even the ups-and-downs of dinner the evening before — had it all lulled her into forgetting the early antagonism between them?

Her eyebrows went up.

'Keeping an eye on me, Rafe? Making sure I don't go near your car and nobble it a second time?'

She saw a hint of colour stain his cheeks and knew she was right.

'Perhaps,' he acknowledged, meeting her gaze evenly. 'Or perhaps, Lau-ren,' he went on, his beautiful voice lingering over her name in the way that melted her bones every time, 'perhaps I'm looking forward to a morning spent in your company.'

A Second Act Of Sabotage

It was not yet nine, but the sun was already warm on their backs as Lauren and Rafe made their way across the square, looking for Dave's Austin Seven. Lauren had slung navy overalls over one shoulder and held a small pouch of tools. She guessed Rafe had something similar in the backpack he carried.

They walked side by side, not touching, the silence between them broken every now and then by brief, terse comments on what was happening around them.

Cars were arriving from all over France and beyond. Lauren saw Dutch and Belgian number plates, German ones, too. Rafe asked a marshal what time they should move their own cars into place. The official beamed at Lauren and held up both hands, fingers splayed.

'*Dix heures*.' Ten o'clock.

Lauren laughed.

'I obviously look very British.'

'You do,' Rafe murmured, and there was a softness about his tone that made her heartbeat give a little leap. She twisted round to look at him. His expression was blandly neutral.

She was at a loss, unable to read the man. Too many conflicting thoughts were speeding through her. Was she to take at face value his assertion that he wanted to spend time with her, unlikely though it seemed? Or should she trust her instincts that he still suspected her and her sister of sabotage?

Having learned Jessica was spending the morning with Chrissie, had he concluded he only had to keep an eye on Lauren? And had he put on old work clothes because he could be pretty sure she'd be working on cars that morning and, dressed appropriately, he could stick close to her?

She puffed out a breath. Or was that just far too far-fetched? Was she guilty of overthinking the whole situation?

Perhaps the best idea was simply to enjoy the morning with Rafe — but remain wary.

It was with something close to relief that she spotted a couple of familiar faces at the foot of the bandstand.

'Look, there's Aurélien. And the deputy mayor. One of the rally organisers. Let's go and say hello.'

There were handshakes and smiles all round with the deputy mayor, Aurélien and the three men standing with them.

'Ah, you British,' the deputy mayor said in his strongly accented English, holding on to Lauren's hand. 'You are winning our best of show prize too often. Don't you agree, Aurélien?'

Was it Lauren's imagination, or was there a hint of anger behind the smile? Perhaps Rafe heard it, too, for she sensed something more than casual interest in the question he asked.

She could make out the words 'Renault' and 'Landaulette' in the other man's reply, but the men were speaking French and she couldn't follow the rest.

'The deputy mayor,' Aurélien explained in his careful English, 'is saying he has finished restoring the old 1931 Renault KZ Landaulette he was working on last year. He, too, will be hoping for a chance to win the prize.'

'As will you with your beautiful Lancia.'

Aurélien dipped his head in the smallest but most graceful of bows.

'Yes indeed, *mademoiselle*.'

'Hmm,' Rafe murmured moments later when they'd said their goodbyes and were heading off. 'Not a disinterested organiser, our deputy mayor. He's out to win that prize.'

Lauren laughed.

'He's not the only one. It's a lot of money.'

They found Dave and Sarah on the terrace of the Café des Sports. Rafe shook Dave's hand and kissed Sarah on the cheeks. It was a touchy-feely custom Lauren hadn't really been aware of the year before, too wrapped up, perhaps, in her increasingly unhappy relationship with Patrick. But she rather liked it, she decided, giving both her friends kisses on the cheeks.

'Listen, Lauren,' Dave said. 'We're waiting for a video call from Sarah's mum. Do you mind having a look at the engine by yourself?'

'No probs. OK if Rafe has a look too?'

'Oh. Yes. Yes, of course. Here, take the key, in case you want to start her up.'

The car was parked in the shade of a lime tree. Rafe ran his fingers along the top edge of the door.

'The bodywork's in beautiful condition.'

'Courtesy of Nichols Classic Cars.' It was impossible not to let a hint of pride enter her voice.

She felt colour warm her cheeks, and she dipped her head, busying herself releasing the catch down near the wheel arch and lifting half the bonnet up and over. Rafe came to join her, and the two of them peered down at the motor.

'The engine's a bit rough and rattly,' Lauren said. Rafe was so close his arm was brushing against hers.

'Dave's thinking tappets.'

'Or it could be a problem with the camshaft.'

'That's right. So, let's have a look.' And she reached down into the engine compartment, checking bolts, clips and wires to see if anything was loose. Very soon they were taking it in turns to reach down into the small space, checking over every part of the engine.

Lauren was smiling, relaxed. The two of them were working in harmony together. That feeling of closeness, of something shared, was back.

That dangerous feeling, one part of her cautioned. Did she dare risk Rafe coming to mean far more to her than she did to him?

Yes, she thought. Enjoy it while it lasts!

The job was finally finished, and Lauren brought the bonnet back down.

'Nothing obviously wrong,' she said, wiping her hands on a cloth before passing it to Rafe. 'You've got grease on your T-shirt.'

'So have you. We should have put

overalls on after all.'

She smiled.

'We make a good team, you and I.'

'You certainly know your stuff. Tell me —' Handing the cloth back, Rafe leaned back against the Austin's gleaming red bodywork. 'Working with cars, it's an unusual career path for a woman.'

Lauren too leaned back against the side of the car, next to him.

'You're forgetting, it's a family business. Jess and I knew, right from when we were very young, that one or both of us would go into it — and take over when Dad retired.'

'I can't imagine Jessica brandishing a torque wrench.'

Lauren laughed.

'Not quite her style, eh?'

But Rafe must have heard something strained in her laughter or her tone for he part-turned towards her.

'What is it, Lauren?' he asked quietly.

She looked down at her hands and saw a line of dirt under one of her nails.

Sudden tears misted her eyes.

'I suppose I have a love-hate relationship with my sister.' She faltered. The emotions the subject aroused were so painful, she rarely spoke of it, hardly ever admitted it, not even to herself.

'Go on.' Rafe's tone was gentle, encouraging.

'Jessica's beautiful, clever, creative . . . all the things I'm not,' Lauren found herself saying.

'I'd dispute that.' His voice was a growl.

'Lauren, you —'

'I'm not fishing for compliments, Rafe. And I don't want your sympathy.'

She pushed herself fully upright, found Rafe had done the same and was taking her hands in both of his, drawing her close.

'I was the same, you know,' he said. 'Elodie, my sister — she's two years older than me. She was always the clever one, getting top marks in all her tests, while I only did well at the subjects that interested me.

'The teachers were always going on at me about Elodie. 'Why can't you be more like your sister?' 'She learns her lessons.' 'She does her homework.' I just knew they were comparing me all the time — unfavourably — to her.'

'Oh, Rafe.' Her heart went out to him. She knew exactly what he meant. 'They probably weren't, though. Comparing the two of you, I mean.'

'I'm not so sure. Some were. But you're right — most of the time it was all in my head.' He sucked in a breath. 'Elodie took the usual academic path — lycée, followed by uni.

'I, on the other hand, partly from choice, partly because my marks weren't high enough, took a longer, more round-about way to get to the same level.'

'A technical, more practical route?' His closeness, the warm strength of his hands round hers, the citrus tang of the soap he used, were making her breath-less.

He nodded.

'The thing is, I wasn't comparing

like with like.' His grip on her hands tightened. 'We're two completely different people, my sister and me. One of us isn't better than the other. We're just — different.' Releasing one of her hands, he reached up to brush a strand of her hair back from her face. 'And it's the same with you and your sister.'

'Ever since I can remember —' Her voice caught, and she wasn't sure whether it was his words or the touch of his fingers on her face that caused it. 'I've always thought I'd never measure up to her.'

'Lauren —' Emotion darkened Rafe's features, and he gathered her to him, wrapping his arms round her, drawing her head against his shoulder. 'Never think that.' He spoke into her hair, and his voice was muffled.

'You may not want compliments, but I'll say it anyhow. You are beautiful, Lauren. And a success. In your chosen field you're a success. Don't ever think anything else.'

'It isn't easy.'

'I know.'

She could stay here for ever, she thought, here in the warmth of Rafe's arms. He held her tight still, hands stroking her back as he murmured soothing sounds into her hair, and it was as if she'd found a kind of inner peace.

'Hey, mustn't disturb the lovebirds.'

It was Patrick.

Rafe's arms tightened around her just as she pulled herself free. She whipped round, her back to Patrick, her only thought to stop him seeing her face, and cuffed the wetness from her cheeks. Turning back, she saw Rafe giving her ex the briefest of handshakes.

'Patrick,' he said, expression cold. 'Come to tell us it's time to move our cars?' As he spoke, he looked towards Lauren behind him and reached out, grasping and letting go of her hand, his eyes meeting hers in a question.

She nodded, his concern bringing fresh tears to her eyes. Behind Patrick, she could see Dave followed by Sarah, beaming a smile. A hopeless romantic, she was no doubt already planning the engagement party menu.

'They want us to put the British cars over by the church,' Patrick was saying, 'and that's good. We'll be in the shade from about midday on.'

Dave gestured towards his Austin.

'Thanks, Lauren. And Rafe. Let me know how much I owe you.'

'Don't be silly, Dave,' Lauren said. 'It was a pleasure.'

She and Rafe picked up their bags and the overalls they hadn't used, and headed back the way they'd come earlier that morning, taking a zigzag path round people and beautiful old cars.

The owners of some of them stood beside their vehicles, ready to answer questions. The rally was clearly going to attract a large crowd, and Lauren was pleased. It had been popular the year before, too.

They walked in silence until Rafe spoke.

'Was Patrick like that when he was with you? Controlling?' There was a hard edge to his voice. When Lauren didn't reply straight away, he went on. 'I was thinking of the meal last night — when he said he wanted Chrissie to eat — normally.' He almost spat the last word out. 'So, was he?'

Lauren sucked in a shaky breath.

'Yes. He was. I didn't realise it at first. It was slow, a drip drip process. The jeans I was wearing weren't quite right. The hairdresser hadn't made a good job of my hair. Things like that. Little things. But they wear you down, sap your confidence. And when you haven't got much confidence to start with . . .' Her voice trailed away.

Rafe surprised her by putting his arm round her shoulders, pulling her to him.

'Patrick's an idiot,' he said. 'You're well rid of him.'

They'd arrived at their cars. Rafe crossed to his Bentley and Lauren to the Riley. Leaves had fallen from the lime tree into the car, and she picked them out. A grasshopper, too — vivid green against the red upholstery — sat motionless on the back seat.

Lauren cupped her hands round the creature and lifted it up and out of the car and down to the ground — and that was when she saw it — a patch of wet in the sandy gravel. She wouldn't have thought twice about it, but it stood up in miniature mountain peaks as though someone had pushed at the gravel with their shoe in an attempt to cover the wet up.

She frowned, suddenly uneasy. Why would anyone do that? Why would anyone bother?

Crouching down, she was tempted to scoop some of the sand and gravel up on her fingertips in order to smell it. Best not, though: a dog, or the fox she'd seen the night before, might have passed that way — although, again, why would anyone bother to cover the evidence up?

The wet patch was near the back of the car. Still crouched, she twisted round, running her fingers along the spokes of the rear wheel, round the tyre, under the wheel arch. Standing up, she examined the folded-down hood, and twisted the petrol caps — but they remained firmly closed. There was nothing unusual, nothing out of place, nothing wet — yet Lauren's unease persisted.

She glanced across to see Rafe about to climb into the Bentley. The cars had to be in place by ten. She ought to get moving. Getting into the Riley, she turned the key and pressed the starter button.

The engine caught, spluttered — and died.

Fresh unease stirred. The Riley normally started first time. She tried again. The engine caught, its usual regular rhythm now ragged, uneven. Lauren looked to the rear of the car. A cloud of white was coming from the exhaust.

She felt her stomach lurch. She knew what it meant. Heart thudding, she snapped the key round to off.

'Water.' Rafe didn't make it a question. His expression was grim as he left the Bentley and came towards her.

'Yes.' She nodded. 'There's something

you ought to see —' Pushing the door open, she scrambled out, went round the back of the Riley and showed him the wet patch. 'They spilled some.'

Now she understood why someone had scuffed sand and gravel over that patch, trying to hide it. Trying to hide the fact they'd put water in the petrol tank.

Rafe was taking his phone out of his pocket.

'She'll need to be towed.'

'Yes.' Watching as he brought the phone up to his ear, listening as he spoke in French, she felt numb. This couldn't be happening. Rafe had been right all along. What had occurred with his car hadn't been an accident, or due to carelessness on his part.

And what was happening now was surely a second act of sabotage.

Rafe closed his phone.

'They're sending a breakdown truck straight away. It'll be here any minute.'

'Good.' She turned away, hugging her arms across her chest. 'Rafe, I don't know what's going through your mind but —'

Close to tears, she faltered, swallowed, pushed on.

'I hope you don't think this is some crazy double bluff where I damage my car in order to prove —' She turned back to face him again, uncrossing her arms to sketch speech marks in the air. 'To prove I'm not the saboteur — even though I am.'

He was shaking his head, had been shaking it from the moment she said 'double bluff'.

'No, Lauren, *ma chère*, I don't think that,' he said quietly.

A loud, repeated beep-beep announced the arrival of the breakdown truck. With Rafe at her side, she watched in silence as the vehicle reversed on to the square and backed up to her car.

The driver jumped out of his cab and shook hands with the two of them, then lowered the sloping ramp, hooked the Riley up and set the winch in motion.

'I'll fill him in on what we think has

happened,' Rafe said.

Fighting back the tears, Lauren expelled a juddering breath as she saw Rafe speak to the driver, and followed the car's slow passage on to the truck.

The Riley had always had a special place in her heart, ever since the day she'd found it, a rusting hulk, under a tarpaulin in a barn. She'd lavished care and attention on it, restoring it to gleaming, smooth-running perfection.

'I don't think I've done any permanent damage,' she said, voice thick, when Rafe came to stand at her side again. 'I only had the engine on for a few seconds.'

The water, she knew, would have settled at the bottom of the petrol tank and would therefore be drawn into the fuel lines before the petrol, diluting it and making it impossible for the motor to function properly.

Rafe's expression was serious.

'He says the car won't be ready before Monday lunchtime at the earliest,' he said, putting his arm across her shoulders, drawing her to him.

'Monday? But that's when we're sup-posed to get the ferry back home.' It was an effort to speak, to hold back the tears. The garage would flush the petrol and water from the fuel tank and engine, and dry it all out, an operation that required specialist equipment — and time. 'I'll have to re-book.'

At last the Riley was in place. The breakdown truck moved off.

'She looks so tiny, so fragile.' Lauren watched until the vehicle turned on to the road and trees hid it from sight.

'Oh, Rafe — she's out of the running, isn't she? I won't be taking part in the rally.'

The tears came then, and she turned, burying her face in his chest. She felt his arms come round her, holding her tight, heard the soft soothing words he mur-mured.

For the second time that day, Rafe was holding her, comforting her. And it seemed the most natural thing in the world.

Danger In Their Midst

Lauren's heart was heavy when at last she pulled away, turning her back on Rafe, knuckling the tears from her cheeks. People looked at her as they passed by, and she guessed her eyes were red-rimmed, over bright.

'We've got to phone round,' she said. 'Get everyone together. Warn them — oh!'

She looked over her shoulder at Rafe, saw him push his fingers through his hair, and knew he'd already got this far in his thinking.

She closed her eyes, and shook her head. She'd never felt so wretched. The exciting trip to France in her beloved classic car, in the company of like-minded friends, was turning into a nightmare.

'What happened to my car — it could have been anyone here.' Her sweeping gesture took in the whole of the square and the people all around. 'I'm right, aren't I?'

Rafe nodded. His mouth and the line of his jaw were hard and unyielding, but the expression in his eyes was one of unhappiness, and she knew he didn't relish the truth any more than she did.

'But what happened to *your* car,' she said, 'could only have been done by someone on the ferry. Possibly someone we don't know about who was on the boat at the same time.'

The suggestion was unlikely in the extreme. She knew she was clutching at straws. But the truth was almost too unwelcome to face.

'Or, more likely,' she said, 'it was one of us.'

Rafe pushed his hands in his pockets and looked away.

'We've been lucky. The damage has been to cars, not to people. But some-one might get hurt next time.'

'Next time?' Lauren felt her stomach lurch. 'You think there'll be a next time?'

'We don't know who's doing this. We don't know why. Maybe there won't be a next time. But I don't think we can take the risk, do you? We should call the gendarmes.'

Lauren didn't respond straight away, turning instead to look around her. Even though it was only Friday morning and the rally hadn't yet begun, the square was filling up.

Cars painted in eye-catching reds and yellows and greens, or glossy black or blue, were parked in rows, some in the shade of trees or buildings, others in the full glare of the sun.

People strolled between them, running their fingers along the bodywork, chatting with drivers, taking photos.

On the face of it, it was a normal, happy scene at a normal, uneventful rally, the sort of thing she went to several times each year. Yet this time it was different.

Lauren sucked in a shaky breath. She was torn. Her rational self understood Rafe's logic. But in her heart of hearts she couldn't accept that one of the group was responsible for what had happened.

They were her friends. She knew them too well. Could one of them really have sabotaged two cars?

Her gaze went from a woman pushing a buggy to a man with a spanner in his hand, and on to an old man leaning on his cane. There were so many people here. She almost wished she could declare one of them the saboteur.

She turned back to Rafe.

'Let's get the others together first, tell them what's happened.' Or was that simply putting off the evil moment, she wondered.

'Even if one of them's responsible for it all. Even if it means we're revealing what we know to him. Or her,' she added, as another frightening thought occurred. What if it was Jessica?

'And then maybe, we can call in the gendarmes.'

'I feel it would be a mistake to wait.' Rafe clipped the words out, anger making the French lilt to his voice more pronounced than usual.

Lauren's chin came up.

'They're my friends. They should be given the chance to talk about it. Besides, if we're all together, whoever it is won't be able to sabotage another car.'

'Unless he or she already has.'

'No-one will be driving their car before the concours d'élégance at three. No-one will be in any danger until after that.' Meeting his gaze, she took her phone out of the back pocket of her jeans.

'True.' She saw the tension ease a fraction from Rafe's stance, and he too reached into his pocket for his phone. 'OK, we'll do it your way.'

★　★　★

'I disagree,' Patrick said, looking coldly across the table at Rafe. 'We'd be a laughing stock if we called in the gendarmes. We've only got your word for it that you checked the radiator drain tap on the Bentley.

'You can't be anywhere near a hundred per cent sure that what happened to your car was sabotage. Can you?'

Lauren saw Rafe stiffen. His hands clenched. He paused an instant, clearly thinking back.

'Ninety-nine point nine per cent certain,' he said, 'but not a hundred per cent, no.'

Belle, lying on the ground behind Bob, lifted her head and growled. The meeting was not going well.

There were seven of them sitting on the terrace of the Café des Sports, where they'd pushed three tables together. Jessica and Chrissie would be joining them shortly.

They were at the top of the church tower, and it would take them some time to climb the 365 steps down to the bottom.

'I'm with Patrick on this,' Bob said, pushing his empty coffee cup away. 'None of us speaks or understands French very well.

'I don't want to find myself spending the night in a cell simply because I didn't understand the question, or said *oui* instead of *non*.'

Murmurs of agreement greeted his words.

'There's no argument about what happened to my car, though,' Lauren said. 'It was definitely sabotage.'

The garage had phoned Rafe to say they reckoned close on a litre of water had been poured into the petrol tank.

'No argument, but no proof, either,' Patrick said. 'That's why it makes no sense to bring the gendarmes in. There's no point in them testing for fingerprints, for instance — so many people like to touch the cars.'

'Especially nice shiny chrome bits like petrol caps,' Sarah said.

'Could just have been kids larking around,' Dave added.

'What if the saboteur tampers with the braking system next?' Rafe cut in.

For the space of several heartbeats, there was no reply. The possible outcome was too awful to contemplate.

'We've got to be vigilant,' Dave said. 'We've got to check our cars before driving off anywhere.'

'They must have poured the water in some time during the night,' Sarah said.

'There are too many people around during the day. Maybe we should organise lockable garage space for the cars.'

'Good idea, Sarah, love. Rafe, could you organise that?'

'Of course.'

Brenda puffed out a long, exasperated breath. Belle growled again.

'We're avoiding the elephant in the room, the fact Rafe and Lauren think one of us is behind it all.'

'Possibly behind it all,' Lauren corrected.

She couldn't bear to turn and see the grim expression on Rafe's face as he sat beside her, or the rigid set of his back. She felt beyond wretched. The meeting had been even worse than she'd imagined.

'But don't worry, Bren.' Her voice was thick, and heavy with painful irony. She was close to tears. 'From now on we're all going to be watching each other so closely no-one will ever dare do anything.'

Looking across at the square, she saw Jessica and Chrissie heading towards the café.

'We got here as soon as we could,' Chrissie muttered in response to some comment from Patrick.

Taking a chair from a nearby table and making a place for herself between Lauren and Rafe, Jessica gave her sister's hand a quick, reassuring squeeze.

'OK, Lauren? We'll soon have your car back. You'll see. Everything will be all right.'

Lauren looked at the tight, uneasy expressions on her friends' faces, saw the way they avoided looking at each other or, if caught looking, immediately looked away. The group was fractured by anxiety and suspicion. Questions without answers. Suspicion without justification. Things couldn't possibly be any further from being 'all right', Lauren thought.

'So the majority decision,' Rafe ground out, 'is that we rule out calling in the gendarmes?'

'Agreed.'

'Ye-es.'

'We don't know for sure the two incidents are connected.'

'Lauren?'

She hesitated, torn, all too aware of how she'd once suspected Jessica of tampering with Rafe's car. But there was no way she'd have sabotaged her own sister's vehicle. Was there?

'No gendarmes,' she said unhappily, shaking her head, and found she couldn't meet Rafe's gaze.

'Very well.' The disappointment in his voice was a further pain in her heart. 'I've no doubt you've got your reasons.' He got to his feet, scraping the café chair back across the pavement.

'I must move the Bentley. I'll find out about lockable garage space while I'm about it.'

'I'll come with you.' Dave jumped up. 'I, erm, could do with a walk.'

Lauren sucked in a long shaky breath as she watched the two men disappear into the crowd. Was this how it was going to be from now on? With everyone policing everyone else? Creating mistrust where none had existed before?

Were the two incidents connected, she wondered, frowning. And if so, why? Why on earth would someone want to damage her car or Rafe's?

Questions, questions. Would there ever be an answer?

Rafe and Dave came back, smiling, looking on better terms with each other than when they'd set off.

'We've rented a lockable space big enough for all five cars,' Rafe explained. 'It's over there, the other side of the square.'

'Very near Bob and Brenda's B&B,' Dave said.

There were murmurs of 'Good' and 'Great stuff', and the atmosphere seemed to lighten a fraction.

Even so, lunch was a prickly affair. In unspoken agreement they all stayed together at the café. They sat, though, at three separate tables, and conversation was no more than spasmodic.

Sitting with Sarah and Dave, Lauren darted a glance at the table where

Rafe sat with Brenda and Bob. How she wished she were there with him, tinglingly aware of his closeness, breathing in the light citrus notes of his cologne . . .

Brenda must have caught her glance.

'Poor you, Lauren love,' she called over. 'You won't be taking part in the concours d'élégance, will you?'

'I won't, either,' Jessica piped up from the table she was sharing with Chrissie and Patrick. 'It's such a shame. I've made nineteen-thirties costumes for both of us.'

'Well, there's a surprise,' Bob muttered, though not unkindly.

'Lau-ren can come with me in the Bentley.' Lauren looked from her sister to Rafe Those beautiful eyes of his were fixed on her face, and her heart seemed to miss a beat. 'If you want to,' he added.

Her heart missed another beat.

'I'd like that.' Very much, her senses were singing.

'And Jess can come with us in the Austin,' Sarah said. 'Might be a bit of a squash, though.'

'Before you ask, it wasn't me,' Jessica stated some time later. It was almost two in the afternoon. Like the others in the group, the two of them were walking back to their B&B, intending to get changed into their costumes for the concours d'élégance.

Rafe wasn't with them. Accompanied this time by Bob, he'd gone to collect the keys for the lock-up garage space.

'I didn't put water in your petrol tank.'

'I never thought you did.' It had been a long, harrowing morning, and Lauren was in no mood for any sort of discussion.

'No? Wasn't that why you were reluctant to bring in the gendarmes?'

Lauren felt herself colour.

'Well, maybe.'

Jessica stopped walking, catching her sister's hands in both hers.

'Thanks for thinking of me,' she said quietly. She shook her head, smiling. 'And I know how much you love that

114

car. I know how much work you've put into it. Believe me, I'd never do anything to damage it — or hurt you.'

'I know,' Lauren said, equally quietly, a lump forming in her throat.

They walked on in companionable sisterly silence until Jessica spoke.

'Look, there's something else. I like Rafe. I really do. But you need to be careful, Lauren. We don't know anything about him. Not really. He's a clever man, and — reading between the lines last night — I could see he was determined to get Hennessy Motors back on a sound footing.'

Lauren frowned.

'Of course he is. It's his family's firm. I don't see what the problem is.'

Jessica made a small exasperated sound low in her throat.

'Look, this business about bringing the gendarmes in — did he mean it? He didn't really press his case, did he?'

Didn't he? Lauren thought he had.

'What are you saying?'

'I'm saying —'

But Lauren wasn't listening any more. She knew what Jessica was going to say. She herself had brought the possibility up with Rafe.

A double bluff. What if the story of the Bentley's radiator leak was an elaborate ploy to make it appear he was the first victim of a saboteur when in fact he was the perpetrator, and she was the first victim?

And the motive? The rivalry between the two garages. That made sense, didn't it?

Lauren stopped so suddenly the couple behind bumped into her. Appalled at herself, she stared at her sister. What was she thinking of?

For one brief fraction of a second she'd been ready to believe that, yes, Rafe had concocted such an underhand scheme, had sabotaged her car.

But this was the man she had grown to know. And to like. More than like, if she was totally honest with herself. How, then, could she have doubted him — even for an instant?

In His Kiss

A hot shower always worked wonders, Lauren decided. With a contented sigh, she closed her eyes, loving the feel of the water as it hit her head and shoulders and flowed down her body. For a few short minutes she could forget everything that had happened, give herself over to pure sensation.

But as she towelled herself dry, the suspicions, the unanswered questions, resurfaced, itching at her consciousness. Who? Why?

Dave or Bob? With or without their wives? Surely not. She'd known the four of them first as clients of Nichol's Classic Cars. Since then, they'd become firm friends. They'd never dream of damaging her car. Would they?

Patrick? Lauren paused to consider. A more likely candidate, she conceded, conscious of the antagonism between him and Rafe. Two alpha males, battling it out. Or rather, one alpha male — Patrick — afraid of losing his position to the other, and fighting back?

Had he observed the closeness she'd shared at times with Rafe — and somehow been jealous? Was that why both her car and Rafe's had been targeted?

She shook her head. No. Patrick was controlling, he had to be in charge. But he hurt with words, confidence-sapping words. Devious, hidden actions weren't his style.

OK, so why? Lauren tugged a comb through her wet hair. Was the motive personal? Someone wanted to hurt both her and Rafe?

But that didn't make sense, did it? Two days before, they'd never even met.

Were these random acts? Or had there been other incidents of sabotage? Perhaps the next step should be to talk with the rally organisers.

Feeling a shade more positive, Lauren let herself out of the steam-filled bathroom.

'Hey, you took your time,' Jessica said, but her tone was good-natured rather than critical.

Sitting in one of the two armchairs by the window, she got to her feet as her sister came into the room and tucked her sketchbook down the side of the chair.

She'd changed into a long narrow dress — another of her own creations. The silky, sunshine-yellow fabric was cut on the bias, hugging her tall, slender frame, and she looked simply stunning.

'I was thinking,' Lauren said.

'Yes, there's a lot to think about,' her sister agreed. 'But leave it for later. Right now, dry your hair and I'll show you what I've made for you.'

It was a sailor suit — but no ordinary sailor suit. Jessica had fashioned navy and cream vertically striped fabric into wide-legged trousers with a high waist and button-up flap front, while the close-fitting top was plain navy with one of those wide square cream collars Lauren had seen in films and photos of sailors from the war.

'And the shoes,' Jessica said.

Two-tone, in navy and cream. Lauren

loved them instantly.

'Look in the mirror. Go on,' Jessica urged, placing a dixie cup cap at an angle on her sister's head and fastening it with a couple of grips.

'Very nineteen-thirties,' Lauren managed, gazing at her reflection, almost lost for words. Her clever sister's outfit gave her height and subtly emphasised her curves. She looked — yes — that was the only word for it: feminine.

'Thank you.' She pulled Jessica into a hug as tears sprang into her eyes. 'It's gorgeous.'

'Good. I'm glad. Come on. We must go.' Pulling away, Jessica put her own hat on, a small rounded felt, sunshine yellow like her dress, and the low-heeled shoes she slipped on her feet.

There was a definite buzz in the air, even though it wasn't yet three in the afternoon and the judging wouldn't begin until four. An electric mix of excitement and tension, Lauren thought as she and Jessica let themselves out of the B&B and made their way across the square.

Owners stood next to or sat in their cars, almost all of them dressed in clothes appropriate to the age of their vehicle. Members of the public crowded round, asking questions, moving from one car to the next. Stalls sold wine by the glass, or sausage-filled baguettes, or nougat in cellophane wraps, the foods for sale filling the air with their scents.

The sun was hotter than ever on their backs, and Lauren was glad of the shade the lime trees provided — and of the light airiness of the costume her sister had made for her.

'There's the Austin,' Jessica said, pointing through the trees.

'Hey, you two are looking great,' Lauren said with a laugh moments later. Sarah was wearing a neat, knee-length floral print dress topped by a small felt hat perched on top of her head while Dave had dressed in a collarless white shirt with the sleeves rolled up, and baggy brown trousers held up by purple braces.

'Wow, how about you, Lauren — you're looking fabulous.'

There was no doubting Sarah's sincerity, and Lauren felt emotion tighten her chest.

'It's all Jessica's doing. My clever sister designed and made it for me.' She stopped, suddenly reluctant to think about what came next. 'Well, um, I suppose I'd better find the Bentley. And Rafe.'

She barely saw the cars she moved past. She was walking slowly, she realised, and knew why — she didn't want to face Rafe Corsini. She couldn't forgive herself for accepting — even for one brief moment — that he might be the saboteur.

He was standing beside the Bentley, talking to an elderly couple, and her breath caught in her throat. He hadn't seen her, and for long seconds she simply stood there, in the shade of the lime tree, watching him.

Wearing a dark grey suit with fine lighter grey stripes, a grey fedora with a wide lilac ribbon band on his head, he looked superb — and every inch the 1930s gangster.

She could watch him for ever, she thought, smiling, taking in his height and the breadth of his shoulders, and the expressive way he moved his hands when he spoke.

The elderly couple glanced her way. He part-turned, caught sight of her, and the smile that lit his face sent her heart soaring.

He tipped the brim of his hat towards her and murmured something to the couple who shook hands with him and nodded to Lauren as they went on their way.

All at once, she felt awkward, her sister's doubts about him, her own brief acceptance of those doubts far too vivid in her mind.

'You scrub up well,' she said as he drew near. The light, jokey laugh that accompanied the words sounded brittle and false. His smile faltered and she felt even more wretched.

'We're both favouring stripes, I see.' He was frowning, his gaze searching her features.

'And two-tone shoes.' She bit her lip and glanced down, unable to look him in the eyes.

'Lau-ren. Tell me what's wrong.'

She heard the concern in his voice and the bone-melting way he said her name, and almost confessed. But she shook her head instead.

'Nothing. Nothing's wrong.

'So what do we do?' Again, that bright brittle edge to her words. 'Sit in the Bentley? Drape ourselves over the bonnet?'

'Neither. The judges won't get to us till about five. So —'

All at once, Lauren found herself brightening.

'So we could go round the square, look at some of the other cars.'

'Exactly.' He smiled, and she couldn't help smiling back. 'I'll just ask Bertrand,' he indicated the man sitting behind the wheel of the lovely old Citroën Rosalie that was next in the line of cars, 'if he can keep an eye on the Bentley.'

Yes, of course, Lauren thought sadly as she half-listened to the exchange in French between the two men. Her car was out of action. But for Rafe, sabotage was still a real possibility and he was taking it seriously, further proof — if she'd needed it — that he was not the saboteur.

'This way,' he said. Hooking his arm round hers, he drew her close to his side, and they set off.

She and Rafe were getting into character, that was all, Lauren told herself, the gangster walking arm in arm with his moll. But she was conscious of his closeness and the soft, warm feel of the fabric of his jacket against the bare skin of her forearm.

From time to time, she'd glance up at him, he'd meet her glance and smile — and her heart would skitter into a faster beat.

They listened to owners' stories, looked under bonnets, admired immaculate engines and gleaming bodywork.

And once again Lauren marvelled at the sense they were on the same wavelength. She found herself relaxing, giving herself over to the pleasure of his company.

They came across Bob and Brenda who were also strolling around, looking at the cars.

'And don't you two look a treat,' Brenda said, a broad smile creasing her face as she looked Lauren and Rafe up and down. Belle barked, once, as though asking to be stroked.

'You're looking rather good yourself, Bren,' Lauren said, her friend's comment causing warmth to steal up over her cheeks. 'Bob, too. Your costumes are perfect. Do a twirl, Bren, go on,' she urged, reaching down to stroke the dog with the hand that wasn't curled round Rafe's arm.

Brenda laughed as both her pony tail and her full skirt swirled out, the skirt revealing the layers of stiffened tulle beneath.

Bob's costume, too, an open-necked short-sleeved shirt over loose denim jeans, and his Elvis-lookalike hairstyle, were totally in keeping with the couple's 1950 Roadster. All three — Bob, Brenda and Belle — wore a red-and-white gingham scarf, folded into a triangle and tied round their necks.

'What about Chrissie and Patrick?' Lauren asked. 'Are they in costume?'

Bob shrugged.

'Haven't seen them. But Aurélien's over there.' He pointed to a stand selling candy floss. 'The other side of that. Why don't you go and say hello?'

Aurélien, inevitably, was polishing the mirror-like perfection of his Lancia's midnight-blue bodywork. He wore a suit similar to Rafe's but in brash 1920s colours, the amber stripe that ran down the dove grey cloth picked out again in the ribbon band of his fedora. He straightened when he saw them approach.

'You certainly look the part,' Rafe said, smiling.

'This suit and hat? My wife's last gift to me before she bunked off back to the UK. Taking our son with her.'

Bunked off? Lauren's eyes widened a fraction. Aurélien's speech was usually so precise, so careful, the slang expression jarred.

'I only get to see him during the holidays,' he was saying, 'and even then, she makes it as difficult as possible.'

'He's taken the divorce so hard,' she said to Rafe when the two of them moved off again. 'I feel really sorry for him.'

'He's very bitter still.'

'It can't be easy for him, only seeing his son during the school holidays.' She looked round. 'Where are we going?'

They were on the edge of the square. The cars were all behind them. Lauren could see their B&B over on the right, and the Café des Sports, its terrace crowded with people, immediately in front.

'I got up early this morning, went exploring. I'd like to show you what I discovered.' He twisted round a little, placed his free hand over hers. 'If you're OK with that?'

She didn't hesitate.

'Of course.' She smiled. 'Sounds intriguing.' A pulse of excitement was coursing through her. At the same time, though, she realised, she felt perfectly safe with him.

The two of them turned into the street that ran down the side of the café, leading away from the centre of town. They walked side by side still, arms linked, very close, and Lauren was all too aware of the lean strength of Rafe's body and the elusive citrus notes of the soap he used.

The hand that wasn't hooked round her arm still rested over hers, and she didn't mind. She didn't mind in the least.

The streets were much emptier here. Every now and then, they passed people or cars going in the opposite direction, heading towards the square and the rally.

Three elderly women had brought dining-room chairs out on to the pavement and were sitting there, faces turned up towards the sun. A youngster, barely in his teens, revved his moped before roaring off.

They turned a corner — and all at once they were in a different world. The houses were behind them now. The cars and lorries on the main road were no more than a distant hum. Ahead lay an expanse of grass, sloping downhill, giving way after 20 metres or so to woodland.

'Notre-Dame-des-Bois means Our Lady of the Woods,' Rafe explained, leading Lauren along the path that cut across the grass. 'There are the woods that gave the town its name. There's a shrine inside somewhere, but I haven't found it yet.'

It was the quiet that struck Lauren first, that and the sunlight that filtered between the leaves of the trees, playing over Rafe's features in a way that made her breath catch.

The path they were following narrowed and he let go of her arm, taking her hand instead as he led the way, drawing her along behind him.

'Not much further,' he said. 'Here we are,' he added, moments later.

It was a complete surprise, a river crossed by a low stone footbridge.

'Madame Lepage says it dates back to Roman times,' Rafe said.

And Lauren could believe it. She walked halfway across and stood there, forearms resting on the parapet, Rafe at her side, and stared down at the river.

Circles rippled outwards as a fish came to the surface, then with a soft plop bobbed below again. Bright sapphire-blue damsel flies hovered before darting away. A rustling on the bank, and Lauren glimpsed a shy water vole.

'It's beautiful,' she breathed. 'Thank you, Rafe, for bringing me here, showing me this.'

She fell silent, senses attuned to the warmth of the sun on her skin, the rich complex song of a blackbird close by — and above all, to the presence of the man at her side.

'Rafe,' she began, hesitating, not sure she was doing the right thing. 'Jess and I were, um, discussing things. Earlier on. What had happened to my car. And to yours.'

She stopped, aware he'd turned his head to look at her. But she couldn't meet his gaze, and kept her eyes fixed on the water.

'Go on,' he urged quietly.

'The thing is, I — just for a moment, I was ready to accept you'd sabotaged my car — and I — I feel awful about it.'

'Lauren —' he cut in, but quietly still. Reaching out, he touched a finger to her chin, tilting it round so that she faced him. She was surprised to see warmth, not censure, in his gaze as it moved from her hair to her eyes to her mouth.

'You know,' he said with soft intensity as he bent his head to hers, 'there's an openness about you, an absence of guile, that I —' his pause was infinitesimal '— that I rather like.'

And his lips met hers with a gentle sweetness that set her pulses singing through her veins. She made a small moan of pleasure and his hands were at her back, gathering her up against him, drawing her in close, and she gave herself over to his warmth and strength, the delicious rasp of his jaw against her skin, and the exquisite beauty of his kiss.

A No Win Situation

Long minutes passed before Lauren finally, reluctantly, drew back. Breathless, she saw the colour that stained Rafe's cheeks, and it crossed her mind that if she had a mirror, she'd see the same colour on her own cheeks. His hands were at the small of her back. Her heightened senses could feel them, warm and firm, through the thin fabric of her sailor top.

'Rafe, what's the time?' she said — and was instantly annoyed with herself. Practical as ever. Typical Lauren.

He smiled a slow smile that crinkled the corners of his eyes, and she thought her bones would melt. His hand moved from her back, reaching up to tangle in her hair, and her lips parted as she leaned her head into his palm.

The low coo-coo of a dove came to her through the trees, the blackbird started its sweet song again. Lauren sucked in a breath. She never wanted to leave this place, this magical place.

Rafe bent forward, touching his lips to hers in the lightest of kisses.

'I suppose we ought to be getting back for the judging.'

His hands slid away as he straightened, leaving cool air in place of warmth, and it was as if she'd lost a part of herself.

He took his phone out of his pocket.

'Five past five.'

'We're going to be late.' She didn't mind, not in the least.

'We'll run for it.'

So saying, Rafe took her hand in his and they set off at speed, retracing their steps along the woodland path, across the expanse of grass and back into the streets of the town. Rafe's fedora flew off and they had to stop and go back to retrieve it. He was laughing — it was a madcap race against time, and it was fun.

The three elderly women were still sitting on their dining chairs on the pavement. Lauren beamed them a smile and waved as she and Rafe ran past.

They had to slow right down when they reached the square. Lauren's chest was heaving, but there was no time to catch her breath as they threaded their way as fast as they could between the lines of cars and the crowds of people.

'The rally's certainly popular,' Lauren said. Rafe was still holding her hand, and she loved the feel of it round hers.

They passed Sarah and Dave sitting in their Austin. Jessica wasn't with them but Lauren thought nothing of it — until she and Rafe reached the Bentley.

She jerked to a halt. Jessica was there, leaning back against the driver's side door, beautiful and glamorous and sophisticated — everything that Lauren wasn't — in her clever sunshine yellow dress and matching hat.

'You're too late,' she said. 'The judges have been and gone. Lucky I was here to save the day.'

'What do you mean?' Rafe's voice was a growl, the hand that held Lauren's tight as a vice.

'Whoa!' Jessica's eyebrows shot up.

'Are you accusing me of something?'

'You know what's been happening as well as we do.'

'What might have been happening.'

Lauren frowned. There was something odd, off-key, about her sister's tone and the way she stood. With her hands either side of her hips, palms flat against the Bentley's bodywork, her legs crossed beneath the long, slinky skirt of her dress, she looked for all the world as if she were posing for a glamour shot.

'Why aren't you with Dave and Sarah still?' Lauren asked.

'Bor-ring! Sarah talks of nothing but cakes and quiches. So I came here hoping to see you, and sat in the Bentley when the judges came by.'

Rafe let go of Lauren's hand and crossed the few metres to his fellow countryman Bertrand who stood beside his Citroën Rosalie. Lauren watched him go, saddened, because she knew he was going to check with Bertrand that her sister had done nothing to his car. She saw Jessica was also watching him.

'I won't ask where you've been,' Jessica said. 'Obviously somewhere where the two of you could be alone.'

Sudden heat swept up across Lauren's face. But it was the scornful, needy edge she could hear in her sister's voice that sent a whisper of unease down her spine, an edge that spoke of — what? Jealousy? Unhappiness?

'Jess, what is it? What's wrong?' she said, taking a step towards her sister.

'Nothing.' Jessica's face was without expression. 'The judges thought I looked perfect — absolutely perfect — in the Bentley,' she went on an instant later as Rafe rejoined them.

He put his arm across Lauren's shoulders, drawing her close — an action that earned the hint of a raised eyebrow from Jessica — and gave a barely perceptible nod of reassurance to Lauren.

'So if you get full marks in the concours d'élégance,' Jessica aimed her remark at Rafe, 'you'll know who to thank.'

'I will indeed,' he agreed. 'And, Jessica, if I sounded rather abrupt a few moments ago, I apologise. I hadn't meant to accuse you of anything.'

'I'm glad to hear it.' Jessica's smile, together with the tiny inclination of her head, could only be described as gracious, and Lauren frowned again, puzzled by the theatrical tone and postures her sister had adopted.

Jessica's phone pinged.

'Hah, saved by the bell. Ah, Chrissie's inviting me for apéritifs at the Café des Sports.' She snapped the phone shut. 'Why don't you join us?'

'We will.' Lauren watched her walk away, back straight, head held high, and her heart was heavy. She was in no doubt her sister had been putting on a performance. The question was why? What had she been hiding?

Rafe drew her round to face him, enfolding her in his arms.

'There's something she's not telling us.'

She was worried for her sister, of course she was. But Rafe was holding her in his arms, she could see each thick, curling eyelash, and was all too aware of the salty smell of his skin after their frantic run back to the square, and longed to feel the rasp of his jaw on her face and neck.

She gave no thought to Bertrand, or to the family who had stopped to admire the Bentley. All at once she had just one thing on her mind.

'Kiss me, Rafe,' she whispered.

And he did, a long deep kiss that left her senses both satisfied and clamouring for more.

At last, he drew back. Smiling that slow smile of his, he reached out, smoothing strands of her hair back from her face, then with both hands straightening her dixie cup cap. His own hat now sat at the back of his head. With a laugh, Lauren too reached up to re-set it at its former rakish angle.

He bent forward to kiss the tip of her nose.

'Time for a drink.'

He'd kissed her — twice — that was all, Laura told herself as they walked, taking their time, across the square to the Café des Sports. It wasn't a declaration of love. It didn't mean they'd bonded for life. But the early evening air was still and warm, swifts circled high in the sky, Rafe's arm was heavy across her shoulders — and her senses were singing.

She was bubbling over with happiness, and each time she twisted round to look at Rafe and saw the relaxed lines of his face and the upward curve of his mouth, she could convince herself that he felt the same.

★   ★   ★

As before, three outside tables had been pushed together. The others in the group were all there and had ordered kirs for everyone. Slices of sausage, cubes of cheese and plump black and green olives had been placed in dishes around the tables.

'At least we've had no more incidents with the cars,' Brenda said.

'Santé.' Rafe raised his glass. 'We've

all been vigilant, that's why.'

'Nothing like stating the obvious.' Patrick's tone was so barbed it made Belle growl.

Lauren sent a questioning look at her sister who shrugged. Her ex wasn't sitting next to Chrissie, she saw, and couldn't help thinking the two had had a row. Neither of them was in costume.

The deputy mayor, walking arm in arm with his wife, stopped by their tables and greeted them all.

'Hello again, British,' he boomed in his heavily accented English. 'I hear you have a problem with a car.'

'My car,' Lauren said. It didn't surprise her that he knew. He was a leading light of the town and one of the rally organisers after all. 'Someone put water in the petrol tank.'

'Tsk, tsk.'

'Has there been anything else like that happening, *monsieur*?' she asked.

He shook his head.

'We're renting a lock-up garage,' Sarah said, 'for the next three nights so our cars will be safe.'

The deputy mayor nodded and tapped his ear lobe.

'I hear.' He turned to Rafe and spoke in French. Lauren had no idea what he was saying, but she saw the tightening of Rafe's jaw and knew he was displeased with what he was hearing.

His reply to the other man's remarks was smilingly polite, no more. The deputy mayor's smile was equally tight, and he and his wife left.

'Well,' Bob said, 'what was that all about?'

Rafe puffed out a breath.

'He was saying how insular the British are. You never mingle, he says.'

'What a cheek!'

'Dave, hush. The man's entitled to his opinion.'

'And what did you say?' Patrick broke in. 'You agreed with him, I suppose.' His face was flushed.

Rafe's look was withering.

'I said that events such as this — events that encourage people of different nationalities to mix — could never be a bad thing.'

There were murmurs of 'Hear hear', but inside, Lauren felt sick, hating the atmosphere that had developed. This was what suspicion — ugly, corrosive suspicion — did.

Would the group ever get back the easy camaraderie they'd once shared?

Needless to say, they all went together to fetch the cars and put them to bed for the night. All, that is, except Jessica and Chrissie who opted to stay at the café and have another kir. Further proof, Lauren wondered, that Chrissie and Patrick were less of an item? Did that explain her ex's foul mood?

She hooked her arm though Rafe's as they crossed the square. Her car was out of action, there was no need for her to accompany the others. But she did — because, of course, she wanted to spend every possible, precious moment with Rafe.

Seated beside him, she looked up and around as he drove the Bentley into the space the group was renting. A petrol station and repair shop, empty because the owner had retired and wanted to sell, it was a long, thin building squeezed between the church and a hairdresser's, big enough to garage four or five cars.

She and Rafe were the last to arrive. He turned the engine off, they jumped out — and Lauren was immediately aware of raised voices.

'Arguing about who should be keyholder.' Rafe spoke for her ears alone. Side by side, footsteps echoing from the concrete floor and bare walls, they hurried to join the others who stood in a circle near the large sliding entrance door.

'Squabbling, more like. Like a bunch of kids.' Lauren spat the words out. She was upset and angry. 'There's one way to solve this. Stay here.'

'There's a Latin quote, isn't there?' Patrick was saying, sounding characteristically pompous, as she headed through the door. 'Something about 'who will guard the guards?''

'How about we take it in turns? Dave and me for the first four hours, then —'

'Are you crazy?'

'Swapping over throughout the night? No way.'

Once outside, Lauren ran to the nearest lime tree, broke four twigs off, made sure three were the same length and set off back to the garage, closing her hand round the twigs so only their ends were visible.

Rafe glanced at her hand as she came back in, his mouth curved into a smile, and he gave an almost imperceptible nod. Lauren felt a warm glow steal across her cheeks.

'Car owners will draw lots,' she said. 'Shortest twig wins.'

Yet there were no winners here, she thought sadly. They were friends, a group of friends. But all this bickering and sniping would surely destroy their friendship.

Surprise Confession

'I'll know better next time,' Jessica said, tone heavy with irony as she snapped her sketchbook shut — Lauren caught a quick glimpse of a blank page — jumped to her feet and started undoing the line of hooks and eyes that ran down the side seam of her sunshine yellow dress.

'Know better about what?' Lauren crossed the room and opened the windows, giving the square one last look before she closed the shutters on it.

It was almost midnight. Apart from the Café des Sports where a waiter was stacking the outside tables and chairs, the square was dark and empty.

'I'll know not to bother warning you about a man.'

'Ah.' Rafe. Lauren could feel herself smiling, softening, when she thought his name. She didn't close the shutters after all, but stayed where she was by the window, looking out.

She'd spent the evening with him,

away from the others and their fractious bickering. Long rows of trestle tables had been set out for a dinner in the open air beside the kitchens of the *salle des fêtes*, the assembly hall, and she and Rafe had found two places side by side.

Thinking back, she had no idea what she'd eaten. It had been enough, more than enough, simply being with him, feeling the movement of his arm against hers as they ate, aware of his scent and his closeness.

She couldn't stop looking at him, loved listening to him as he spoke to her or to the people around them, was conscious of the smile that played constantly over her face.

What was he doing right now? They'd kissed one last time on the first-floor landing of their B&B, and she'd watched his long-legged, easy stride as he went along the corridor to his room, blowing her a kiss just before he turned the corner.

Was he too now standing at his window looking out? Was he gazing over the tops of the plum and apricot trees, edged in silver by the starlight, and thinking of her? Was he remembering the kisses they'd shared?

A sudden overwhelming longing to be with him, in his arms, gripped her, and she gasped with the shock of it.

'Hey, what is it?' Jessica was at her side, quickly knotting the belt of her dressing gown. There was concern in her voice, and she put her arm round Lauren's waist, drawing her sister to her. They stood there, together, looking out across the dark square.

'I think I'm falling in love with him.' No need to say who 'him' was.

'I was afraid you might be.' Jessica sighed. Her hand slid away from Lauren's waist, started stroking up and down her arm. 'Promise me you'll take care, Lauren. We know so little about him.'

'Maybe that's true for you, but I feel I know quite a bit about him. We were talking about our future plans earlier on.'

'Oh?' Jessica sent her a narrow-eyed,

speculative look. 'Well?'

'He's really loving the challenge of turning Hennessy Motors around. He's decided to put a manager in charge of his business in Tours and he's going to make the UK his home.'

'Hmm. Even so, if you think about it, it's only since he came on the scene that these weird things have been happening.'

Lauren's heart lurched.

'Coincidence.' It had to be. She'd seen how troubled he'd been by what had happened to his car and to hers.

'I don't want you to be hurt,' Jessica said.

'I won't be. But thanks.'

Neither moved. The late evening air was warm on Lauren's face. Night noises came to her, the call of an owl, the bark of a fox — the fox she'd seen that morning?

Her eyes were adjusting to the absence of light and she could make out the gleam of starlight on chrome and the dark, stealthy shadow of a cat slinking

150

between the cars.

'I, uh —' Jessica cleared her throat. 'I wasn't myself this afternoon.'

Lauren's mind flashed back to her sister's odd, theatrical performance when she and Rafe returned to the Bentley.

'That's right. You weren't.' It had been clear something was wrong, she thought with a guilty pang.

But she'd been so wrapped up in her feelings for Rafe that she hadn't thought to find a private moment later that evening when she could take Jessica to one side and ask her about it.

'Do you want to tell me what it was all about?' she invited.

Jessica didn't answer straight away. Dropping her hands to the window sill, she looked out into the darkness.

'It was Sarah,' she said at last. 'She just had to show me the latest video her mum had sent her. And it showed —' She paused, sucked in a breath. 'It showed little Milo. Of course.'

Lauren heard the smile in her sister's voice, found she was smiling along with her. 'No surprises there.'

'He's learning to talk. And the video shows him toddling along after Sarah's mum's cat, and he's pointing at it and saying 'Ba!'. His version of 'cat'.'

'Yes.'

'And the thing is —' She stopped again, and Lauren could hear the pain that had entered her voice. 'The thing is, I was struck by what a fool I'd been. Why didn't I realise before? A baby is so, so special. Unique.'

'Yes.'

'And I thought: I want to settle down. With Steve. Start a family. More than anything in the world. I want Steve back. I should never have finished with him.'

'Oh, Jess.' Lauren's stomach was swooping, leaving her feeling hollow, sick.

She recalled the weeks of unhappiness Jessica had gone through — Steve, too, she imagined — until a split had seemed the only possible solution. Did Jessica seriously intend reopening old wounds?

'I don't know what to say.'

Jessica laughed harshly.

'Nor do I. I don't know what to think, either. It jolted me so much, I couldn't stay with Sarah a moment longer. That's why I came along to the Bentley. To find you.

'My rational self is telling me I made the correct decision first time round. I'm a career woman — a successful career woman. There's no room for babies in my life. But another part of me —'

Lauren turned towards her, catching her hands in both hers. Tears stung her eyes.

'Listen, Jess, there's no easy answer. But, whatever you decide, it mustn't be a spur-of-the-moment thing.

'You've got a lot of thinking to do, you and Steve. You've got to know you're making the right decision. If there's the slightest doubt, don't do it.'

For a long moment Jessica said nothing.

'You're right of course,' she said finally. 'Wise words. Thank you.'

Lauren gave her sister's hands a

squeeze.

'Come on. It's been a long day. Let's close the shutters and get to bed.'

★   ★   ★

Another troubled night, filled with dreams of Rafe, so intense they made her yearn with longing for him, intercut with the recurring image of a baby girl sitting on a mat, alone and crying her eyes out.

Distressed, Lauren got up when she could bear it no more, opened the shutters and stared out over the square in the cold blue tinge of early dawn. Birdsong filled the air but she scarcely heard it.

She saw the one or two people or vehicles that were out and about at this hour, but her mind was elsewhere.

Lauren wasn't convinced settling down, starting a family, would be the right thing for her sister. As Jessica had said, she'd made the right choice first time round.

It wasn't Lauren's decision to make, of course. She'd support her sister, there was no question about that, but she wouldn't — couldn't — tell her what to do.

With a sigh, she went into the en-suite, showered and dressed in her usual jeans and T-shirt.

Jessica had designed and made her an outfit for the parade through the town and out into the countryside that afternoon. She'd wait until after lunch before changing into it.

Or — the sudden, unwelcome thought struck her — was she taking too much for granted in assuming she'd be in the Bentley with Rafe?

Jessica was up and pulling her dressing gown on when she came out of the bathroom.

'You go on down. Go on,' she said when Lauren hesitated. 'I'm fine.'

She didn't look it. Her cheeks had lost their colour, and there were dark smudges under her eyes.

'Are you sure?'

Jessica's nod was brief, brittle.

'Listen, you won't tell anyone else

what we spoke about last night, will you?'

'No! I'd never do that.'

'Only, Sarah might be a bit curious. I left the two of them rather abruptly.'

'I'll think of something, don't worry.' Jessica smiled.

'Good old Lauren, always so practical.'

Running down the stairs to the dining-room, Lauren gritted her teeth, the word 'practical' ringing in her ears. But halfway down, she realised she actually quite liked being told she was practical.

It was part of her nature, part of who she was. She wasn't ditzy, or purely decorative. She was hands-on. She got stuck in and got things done.

The word no longer had the power to hurt, she realised, and that had to be down to the growing confidence her relationship with Rafe was giving her.

Humming a happy song, she continued on down to the ground floor.

Rafe glanced up as she entered the dining-room, and his face lit up at sight of her. Scraping his chair back across the tiles, he jumped to his feet and came round the table towards her.

He stopped less than a metre away, reaching out to touch his fingertips to her cheek.

'You look lovely.'

'So do you.' It was an effort to breathe. 'Have you been out running?' The salt tang of his skin and the citrus notes of his soap were all around.

He nodded.

'Why not come with me tomorrow?'

'I'd like that.' The touch of his hand as it moved from her face to her ear before tangling in her hair was firm and sure. Images from her dreams the night before flashed into her mind, and hot colour swept into her face.

He bent forward and kissed her on the lips.

'All alone?'

'Jessica's got to do her nails and makeup.'

'Ah. She won't be down for at least an hour then.'

Lauren laughed.

'That sounds about right.'

She sat opposite him so that she had the perfect excuse to keep looking at him. And look she did. He was like a drug fizzing through her veins. She couldn't get enough of him.

They drank Madame Lepage's fragrant coffee, ate buttery croissants and crusty bread, talked about everything under the sun and held hands across the table.

Once again, Lauren marvelled at how completely at ease she felt with Rafe — yet how blisteringly aware of him she was.

Jessica came down at nine dressed in tight-fitting jeans and T-shirt that emphasised her slimness and height. She was wearing heels even higher than those Chrissie had worn the day before and had hidden the dark smudges beneath her eyes with the skilful use of make-up.

But there was something brittle still in the way she flashed her nails as she walked across to the table that told Lauren her sister was putting on another performance, and her heart went out to her.

Rafe shot her a quick frowning glance and she knew he'd seen it, too.

'You're looking bright-eyed and bushy-tailed this morning,' he said, standing up to kiss her on both cheeks.

Jessica laughed.

'Bright-eyed and bushy-tailed? Where on earth does a Frenchman get these quaint expressions from?'

'My English gran,' Rafe said, pouring her a big breakfast cup of black coffee and pushing it across the table to her.

The smile slid from Jessica's face.

'Steve's gran on his father's side,' she murmured, picking her cup up, cradling it between both hands. All at once she seemed to come to a decision. She put the cup back down on the table.

'So, what are the plans for today?' she asked. She sounded brisk, business-like, more like the normal Jessica, and Lauren felt a wave of relief wash over her.

Rafe's eyes had narrowed a fraction.

'We're all due to meet at ten,' he said.

159

'We'll get the cars out of the lock-up garage and out on to the square. After that we'll all head over to the Café des Sports.'

In other words, Lauren thought, everyone would be keeping an eye on everyone else.

'In the afternoon,' she added, 'there's the grand parade through Notre-Dame and out round the surrounding villages.'

And, yes, Rafe did want her to ride in the Bentley with him. Very much, he'd said, and she was conscious of the slow smile that was once again spreading across her face.

'Is your sister all right?' Rafe asked, keeping his voice low. 'Is there something bothering her?'

They'd finished breakfast and were standing in the courtyard outside Madame Lepage's house.

Glancing across at her sister who stood by the front door, her concentration fixed on her phone, Lauren was conscious of the whisper of unease that chilled her skin. Please say she wasn't messaging

160

Steve — it was too soon, she'd given herself no time to think things through.

'Lau-ren?'

'She's fine,' Lauren said, wretchedly aware she couldn't look Rafe in the eyes. 'Shall we go?'

Dave, the key-holder for that night, and Sarah were already there, waiting outside the lock-up garage space. Bob and Brenda, with Belle on a lead, joined them moments later, followed shortly afterwards by Patrick and Chrissie.

'Good. We're all here. Let's get the cars out.'

Dave unlocked the sliding door, Rafe pulled it open, and everyone crowded inside, bending to examine tyres, running hands over bodywork, each checking their own vehicle. To Lauren's relief — to everyone's relief, no doubt — the four cars looked exactly as they had the evening before.

'*Bonjour.* Hello.' The clipped, precise tones were of a voice Lauren recognised. She straightened, looking towards the doorway.

161

'Aurélien, love, great to see you,' Brenda called out, her footsteps echoing on the concrete floor as she crossed over to him. 'What are you doing here? Not that you're not welcome. Come on in. Say hello to the others.'

'I had heard you were keeping your cars under lock and key each night, but I did not know where.'

'So you had a walk round and now you've found us.'

Another round of handshakes and kisses followed.

'We're heading off for the Café des Sports next. Care to join us?'

And so it was arranged. The car owners and their passengers drove their vehicles out of the garage and along to their allotted places while Jessica and Aurélien walked across the square to the café.

Lauren didn't think her sister would want to spend the afternoon driving round the countryside with Dave and Sarah. But perhaps she'd be happy to go with Aurélien in his Lancia.

Worst Fears

The Café des Sports was busy even at this comparatively early hour, but the group had managed to snag their usual tables on the terrace, pushing them together to form one long one. The café owner wound out the awning, shading them from the sun, already warm and carrying the promise of another fine, hot day. The waiter came to take their order.

'That's ten items,' Sarah said. 'It always amazes me how they remember. They never write it down, do they?'

'Training,' Aurélien said. 'In France, waiters are trained. Not so in the United Kingdom, I believe.'

'This is perfect,' Lauren said, sitting back with a sigh.

Rafe, in the chair next to her, agreed. He caught her hand in his, the movement of his thumb slow and sensuous across her palm. Smiling, loving the thrill his touch sent pulsing through her, she watched sparrows flit and hop between the tables, picking up tiny flakes of bread or croissant, and only half-listened to the conversations going on around her.

Belle was lying beside them, chin on her front paws, one eye open. She, too, was watching the birds.

The waiter brought their order. Each cup and saucer came with a couple of sugar cubes wrapped in pink and white striped paper and a biscuit wrapped in clear cellophane.

'There's something printed on here,' Bob said, dropping two sugar cubes into his coffee. 'What does it say?' he asked, holding a candy-striped wrapper out to Rafe.

Letting go Lauren's hand, he sat up, reaching forward to take the small square of paper, quickly scanning it. He smiled.

'It says 'he who laughs at himself never runs out of things to laugh at'.'

'Very funny.'

'Hey, what does mine say?'

''Nothing is impossible to a willing heart',' Rafe read, translating what was written on the second wrapper.

'Oh.' Sarah bit into a biscuit. 'That's rather lovely, isn't it? Can I keep that one?'

'Sure.' Rafe handed it across to her. Reading the wrapper Chrissie passed him, he pulled a wry face.

'This one's a joke. 'My dog used to chase people on a bike'.' He paused. ''It got so bad I had to take his bike away'.'

Everyone groaned and laughed at the same time.

'What does this one say?'

'Here, try this one.'

Rafe read out a motto.

'Don't pursue happiness. Create it.' There were thoughtful murmurs of agreement.

'Do you mind if I keep that one, too?' Sarah asked.

'Ah, this one's untranslatable, I'm afraid.' Rafe was looking at the wrapper Brenda had given him.

'It's a play on words. It only works in French.'

'I know a joke like that,' Dave said. 'How do you know it's been raining cats and dogs?' He paused, looking round at them all. 'You step in a poodle.'

'Dave, that's awful.' Lauren was laughing.

Lauren looked round at the others, at their open, happy, animated faces. Patrick and Chrissie were sitting side by side. He was hugging her to him, a beaming smile on his face. Whatever had happened the day before appeared to have been resolved, and Lauren was glad for them both.

Jessica was laughing, too — and hadn't once looked at her phone since leaving their B&B earlier that morning. Even Aurélien, marginally less formal than usual, seemed to be making an effort to take part.

This was how it should be. This was how she'd envisaged the trip to France — five relaxed, relaxing days in the company of her friends.

The notion of sabotage had taken on an unreal, dream-like distance. She was beginning to wonder whether Patrick had been right. Was it possible Rafe had been careless and forgotten to check the radiator drain tap? Was it possible kids larking about had poured water into her car's fuel tank?

Right at this moment, sitting in the warmth of a July morning in a beautiful part of France, hearing her friends' laughter all around her, she was convinced they'd pushed the two events out of their minds. Perhaps she — and Rafe — should do the same.

Rafe. She breathed out on a long, luxurious sigh. She'd found love during the five-day excursion, and that was a wonderful, unexpected added bonus.

It was the sudden silence that alerted her, bringing her jolting back to the here and now, that and the way Rafe laid his hand across her forearm as though in warning.

She looked up to see Jessica push her chair back and rise to her feet. Chrissie was halfway out of her seat before Patrick caught her round the wrist, restraining her.

Belle sat up and gave a hesitant bark.

Sarah shook her head, looking bewildered.

'I only meant —'

'I'll make my own decisions, thank you,' Jessica said.

It was as if the words were torn from her. Lauren knew her sister wasn't far from tears.

Jessica turned, pushing past chairs, tables and people, and Lauren jumped to her feet.

Rafe's hand slid down her arm, catching her fingers.

'Do you want me to come with you?'

She could see the concern in his eyes, and her throat swelled with emotion.

'No.' With a brief squeeze of his hand, she turned and ran in the direction Jessica had taken, dodging round people, skirting the cars on display. She spotted the back of her sister's head a short distance further on. 'Jess,' she called. 'Stop.'

She'd almost caught up with her when Jessica jerked to a halt.

'Leave me alone.' Her voice was harsh,

strident.

'Tell me what happened, Jess. Please,' Lauren coaxed, taking her sister's hands in both hers, gently pulling her round to face her.

'You're being an annoying little sister. Go away.'

'Jess. Please.'

'I said leave me alone.'

'Jess. Tell me.'

And Jessica's shoulders slumped.

'It was Sarah. Yesterday. I told her why Steve and I split up. A mistake. I shouldn't have done.'

The tear-charged words spilled out, and Lauren's heart ached, sharing her sister's pain.

'Go on,' she said. 'But only if you want to.'

'Sarah must have seen something in my reaction to the video of little Milo following the cat, put two and two together — and made five.'

Lauren frowned.

'And?'

'And she said I should take heed

of the motto. The sugar cube motto. 'Don't pursue happiness. Create it.' She said I should be pro-active — her words — phone Steve and tell him what I was feeling.'

'Oh, Jess.' Yet again, Lauren was at a loss for words. What could she possibly say to comfort her sister? What advice — if any — could she give her?

'You were right. Last night,' Jessica said. 'I've got to think it all through. And for that, dear sister —' She gave the ghost of a smile. 'I need to be alone.'

'Are you sure?' Lauren was reluctant to let her go. 'I could come with you. Keep you company. I won't say anything.'

'No.' The harshness was back. But her eyes were over-bright as she shook her hands out of Lauren's hold. 'Why can't you take no for an answer? I want to be by myself. I'll see you at lunchtime.'

She'd taken no more than a few steps when she stopped and turned.

'Do you think I made the right decision, Lauren? Splitting with Steve, I mean.'

'It was the right decision at the time. Having a baby — and the effect that might have on your career — was making you so unhappy. But now —' She shook her head. 'I don't know.'

'And that's why I need to be alone. To think it all through.'

Lauren watched as her sister disappeared into the crowd and a small knot of anxiety tightened inside her.

But her sister had been adamant. She wanted to be alone. With a sigh, Lauren turned and headed back to the café.

Rafe had left the others sitting round the three tables and was waiting for her in the roadway outside the café. His hands went to her waist and he drew her to him.

'Is everything all right?' he murmured. 'Are you all right?'

Lauren didn't know whether to nod or shake her head.

'I don't —' Her voice caught. 'I don't know.'

Emotion — pain — crossed his face.

'Lauren.' His hands moved to her shoulder-blades, and he gathered her to him, wrapping his arms around her. 'Don't beat yourself up about it. I'm sure you've done everything you possibly could.' He pressed a kiss to the top of her head.

Sarah was hurrying across the road towards them. Reluctantly, Lauren drew away from Rafe's embrace.

'I'm so sorry, Lauren. Please forgive me. I didn't mean to upset Jessica. In fact —' Sarah gave an embarrassed laugh. 'I'm not even sure what I said that was wrong.'

Lauren managed a smile.

'It's all very raw still. The break-up with Steve and everything. Something you said just — touched a nerve, that's all. Please don't worry about it.'

'If you're sure.'

Lauren saw Sarah's shoulders ease as the tension left her and knew her friend was reassured. If only it were as easy for herself!

'Let's get back to the others, shall we?'

But the fun and laughter of so short a time before was no more. Aurélien was the first to make a move.

'Let me get these.' Standing up, he took a couple of ten euro notes from his wallet and put them down on the table. 'I must check on my car, then go home for lunch.'

He shook Rafe's hand and bent to kiss Lauren on both cheeks, prompting everyone to get to their feet to make their farewells.

With a brisk wave, Aurélien was off, crossing the road to the square.

'I reckon that Lancia of his is in with a chance at the best of show prize,' Bob said.

'I must check the MG's in tip-top condition. You'll come with me, won't you, sweetheart?'

In no time at all, only Lauren and Rafe were left. His hands went to her waist again, pulling her close.

'Hungry?'

She smiled.

'No.'

He was studying her face, his gaze moving from her hair to her eyes to her lips, and his mouth curved into that slow smile that never failed to set her senses alight. Her heart skipped a beat. Several beats.

'I've enjoyed this morning with the others. I really have.' Apart from her worry over her sister. But there was nothing she could do about that right now.

'It'd be great, though, if —' Her voice faltered. She didn't know what she had in mind, knew only she wanted to be alone with this man.

'Let's see what happens,' Rafe said, and that beautiful voice of his made it a promise.

He led her by the hand across the square. They walked as fast as they could, side by side if the crowds allowed it, at other times in single file, only slowing — never stopping — to admire some of the old cars that caught their eye.

Lauren's senses were singing. She didn't know where they were going and didn't ask. She trusted him completely, she realised, and thought it rather wonderful that she could be so trusting even as restless excitement pulsed through her.

They exchanged a friendly *bon appétit* with Bertrand who'd set a small fold-out table with benches between the Bentley and his own Citroën Rosalie and was tucking into his lunch.

Dave and Sarah's Austin was a little further on. With a sigh Lauren touched her fingers to the tyre on the spare wheel. The spat between Sarah and Jessica was like a dark shadow over the morning. Where was her sister now, she wondered, biting her lip.

All at once she frowned — and picked up the pink and white sugar cube wrapper that had been crumpled and thrown on to the Austin's driver's-side seat.

'What's this doing here?'

A rhetorical question. Because she thought she knew the answer. A sense of deep unease was crawling along her spine. She looked at Rafe. His frown, the taut line of his mouth, told her he'd

175

had the same thought.

As one, they moved to the front of the car. Releasing the catch, Rafe lifted and folded the driver's-side section of the bonnet. Licking her forefinger, Lauren dabbed it to one or two of the white crystals that lay scattered round the petrol cap, then brought it up to her lips. She felt sick.

Sweet. The crystals tasted sweet. As she'd expected.

It took just one look at her face, and Rafe knew too. His eyes met hers.

'Sugar,' he growled. 'Someone's put sugar in the petrol tank.'

A Shadowy Figure

'We don't know that for sure. It might be a bluff. Pretend. Scattering a few bits of sugar to —'

Rafe's expression was grim.

'The end result is the same.' He took the sugar cube wrapper from her, smoothed it out, scanned the print. 'A motto. Not one we saw this morning.' Pulling out his wallet, he carefully placed it inside.

'We also don't know how many sugar cubes have been dropped in the tank.'

Lauren closed her eyes for a second or two. She could hear the frantic edge to her words as they spilled out and knew she was close to tears.

'It doesn't make any difference. The car will still have to be towed. The tank will still have to be pumped out.'

The hard set of Rafe's face told her he was as unhappy as she was. It didn't help. She realised that in his mind, it always came back to Jessica. When he caught hold of her hands, she snatched them away.

'Don't say it,' she spat out. 'I know what you're going to say and you're wrong. So wrong.'

Rafe pushed his hands into his pockets, swung away, his back to her, then turned back to face her.

'The wrapper could only have come from the Café des Sports —'

'She didn't do it.'

'She had a falling out with Sarah while we were at the Café des Sports.' He ground the words out. 'And, lo and behold, less than an hour later, it's Sarah's car that's sabotaged.'

'Possibly sabotaged.' Lauren paused an instant, sucked in a breath. 'Look, I admit, it did cross my mind she might have tampered with your car. Because of its associations with Steve. But she told me she didn't, and I believed her. I still do.'

Rafe was shaking his head. Tilting her chin, Lauren ploughed on.

'And she'd never — I repeat, never —

have done anything to my car. We're sisters. Family. OK, we have our moments but —'

Rafe lifted an eyebrow.

'Cynicism doesn't suit you,' she snapped. 'Anyway, I'm not even sure Jessica knows an Austin Seven's petrol tank is kept under the bonnet.'

'Her father, sister and ex-fiancé all work with old cars. Of course she knows. It's the sort of detail she could have picked up at any time.'

'So maybe we should get her over here to answer these accusations for herself.'

'Good idea.'

Frustratingly, Lauren's call went through to voicemail. She left a short message: 'Something's happened. Get in touch asap.'

'Hey guys, what are you doing with my car? Why have you raised — ?'

'You're looking very cross. What's the problem?'

It was Dave and Sarah, each holding a long, part-eaten half baguette. The pungent smells of tuna and mayonnaise billowed around them.

Rafe showed them the sugar wrapper and Lauren pointed out the traces of sugar round the petrol cap.

The colour swept from Dave's face.

'We're going to have to bring the gendarmes in this time. There's definitely something going on.'

Sarah nodded. She looked sick.

'We ought to get the others here, tell them what's happened,' Lauren said.

Sarah and Dave stood between her and Rafe, and she told herself she welcomed the distance she'd put between herself and him.

'I'll contact the gendarmes,' he said.

'Yes, do that,' she agreed, doing nothing to stop the cool formality that had entered her voice. He shot her a narrow-eyed look.

Patrick and Chrissie arrived a quarter of an hour later, Bob and Brenda ten minutes or so after that.

'We've had to cut Belle's walk short,' Bob said. The Labrador whined and gave a single wag of her tail, clearly sensing the group's sombre mood. 'Where's Jessica, Lauren, love?'

Unhappily, Lauren shook her head.

'I left a message.' The gendarmes hadn't arrived yet, either.

She stood a little apart from the others, was aware of Rafe's frequent looks in her direction. There were things she had to say to him. But not yet. Not until the two of them were alone.

'That's a myth, sweetheart,' Patrick was saying to Chrissie. 'Sugar doesn't dissolve in petrol. It just sinks to the bottom of the tank and stays there. So there's no way it can clog up the rest of the motor the moment you turn the engine on. That only happens in books and films.'

'Best to play safe and have it removed, though,' Bob said. 'It could damage the fuel filter.'

'Depends how much.'

'Pouring sand in would have the same effect, sweetheart.'

'Heavens, don't give people ideas.'

Walking slowly, hugging her arms

across her chest, Lauren moved away. The others were bound to start discussing the who and the why some time soon, and she didn't think she could bear the pain if — when — her sister's name came up for consideration.

Or should she stay to defend her? Unease jolted through her. Where was Jessica? Lauren rang her again, got through to voicemail, left another message. She'd stay within earshot of the others, she decided.

What fools they'd been — and she included herself in the assessment. The day before they'd been vigilant, alert to the possibility of sabotage, and had stayed with their cars or seen to it that someone else was keeping an eye on them.

Was it because nothing had happened overnight that they'd relaxed their guard that morning? Rafe hadn't, of course. He was looking her way, a look that held both question and concern.

She turned her back on him. He'd asked Bertrand to keep watch on the

Bentley. But, it seemed, Dave hadn't made similar arrangements, and the other two drivers, Bob and Patrick, probably hadn't, either.

Her thoughts went to the couple of hours spent in the café. It had been such fun — what a pity it had had to end like this.

The sugar cube wrapper they'd found had a motto Rafe hadn't translated that morning. So who had kept their wrapper? Who hadn't passed it to Rafe? She hadn't for one, she thought with a stab of anxiety. Bob had, and so had Dave. Sarah had held on to two.

And what about Jessica?

Lauren puffed out an exasperated breath. What was the point of speculating? The saboteur could have taken sugar cubes from another table. Or from the bowl of them kept on the bar counter.

The gendarmes had arrived, a man and a woman, and Lauren headed back to rejoin the group. She'd expected Rafe would have to translate but to her relief — to everyone's relief, she saw — the woman spoke English.

The two of them examined the petrol cap and the sugar cube wrapper Rafe took out of his wallet, said they would wait for the report from the garage that flushed the contents of the petrol tank out, and took everyone's names and addresses.

'Anyone else with you?'

They all looked at Lauren. She cleared her throat, managing a smile.

'My sister. Jessica Nichols. Same address as me.'

The gendarmes left, Rafe phoned for the breakdown truck, and Lauren tried and failed to contact Jessica again.

'We must go and check up on the MG, sweetheart,' Patrick said.

'Ditto, Bob, love. Come on, Belle.'

The breakdown truck driver, arriving shortly afterwards, jumped down from his cab and shook hands all round, greeting Rafe like an old friend.

It wasn't long before the Austin was hooked up, pulled up the ramp and chained into position on the truck. Sarah's eyes were over-bright, and Dave put his arm across his wife's shoulders.

Lauren, too, had a tear in her eye and she reached out to squeeze Sarah's hand as they watched the breakdown truck ease its way very slowly through the crowd. She knew what her friends were going through. After all, her own car had suffered the same fate only the day before.

'Well,' Dave said when at last the truck had disappeared from view, 'there's no point hanging round here any more.'

Lauren and Rafe were alone at last. She swallowed. The time had come.

'There's something I've got to say.'

He grew still. She sensed he was putting himself on full alert.

'Something I'm not going to like.' It wasn't a question.

She made a small movement of the shoulders, a half-shrug.

'Maybe. I won't be riding beside you in the Bentley this afternoon. I won't be going running with you tomorrow morning. I don't want to go anywhere with you. Not any more.'

Anger was driving her. She recognised that. But it was the right thing to do. It was breaking her heart, but it was the right thing to do.

'This is about Jessica, isn't it?'

'Yes.' Her chin came up. 'My sister hasn't done any of these things. She hasn't sabotaged any cars. But for some reason you simply can't accept that.'

Rafe looked away, into the distance, then looked back at her.

'I've tried.' There was a tautness about him that suggested he was choosing his words with care. 'Believe me, I've tried to keep an open mind. But there's always something — motive, opportunity — that implicates her.'

Sudden tears pricked at Lauren's eyes.

'There are some things you just have to take on trust.'

'Lau-ren, I —' Rafe's voice was gruff. He hesitated a fraction of a second, then his hand went to the back of her neck and he bent to touch his lips to hers in the lightest, most tender of kisses. He drew back, those beautiful eyes of his moving over her face as though committing her features to memory.

'You've made your decision and I must abide by it. But I wish —' His voice caught. 'I'm sorry it had to be like this.'

The pain of it was physical. Lauren didn't think she could bear it a moment longer.

'I'm sorry, too,' she said, her words husky with emotion as she tore herself away.

She went back to the B&B, a wounded animal returning to its bolthole. She had a shower, hoping the hot water would wash away her tears. It didn't.

She paced up and down the bedroom, pushing her fist against her mouth, eyes clouded by fresh tears. The anguish didn't lessen.

At three, she gave herself a stern pep-talk, splashed cold water over her face, and went down to watch the parade through the town.

The previous year, she'd taken part

and had loved every minute of it. This year, it struck her as a special kind of torture.

The old cars were as thrilling as ever. She loved the sound of them, loved seeing gleaming bodywork and chrome that dazzled in the sunlight, knew how much hard work had gone into each restoration.

Caught up in the excitement these old vehicles always provoked in her, she found herself almost forgetting her angry exchange with Rafe, and she waved and cheered as the cars she knew went past: Bob, Brenda and Belle in their Roadster, Patrick and Chrissie in his MG, Aurélien in his immaculate midnight-blue Lancia.

She even had a wave for the deputy mayor in his beautifully restored Renault Landaulette, and another for Monsieur Lepage in his breathtakingly fabulous 1902 Panhard and Levassor.

Almost, but not quite, forgetting. The Bentley was one of the last cars to go past. Standing on the pavement outside the B&B, Lauren watched it approach, and her breathing seemed to slow. Her hands dropped to her sides.

He saw her. Perhaps he'd been looking out for her, she thought — and, foolishly, her heart leaped at the notion. An expression on his face that seemed both taut and blandly neutral, together with a brief nod, acknowledged her presence and then he was past her, disappearing out of sight between lime trees and spectators.

She could have been there with him, she knew, close by his side, touching him, listening to him, sharing it all with him. Tears filled her eyes again and she turned away, heading back into the B&B.

Jessica returned not long afterwards, frowning when she caught sight of Lauren's face.

'Hey, tell me what's wrong,' she coaxed, pulling her sister into a hug.

'Maybe it's for the best,' she concluded when Lauren finished recounting the events of the day, ending with her break-up with Rafe.

Lauren bit her lip and said nothing. It certainly didn't feel that way.

★　★　★

It was close on midnight and dark outside. As she'd done the night before, Lauren stood at the window of her bedroom, looking out.

Once again, the only light came from the Café des Sports where the waiters — two of them this time — were stacking the outside tables and chairs. The painted metal of the bandstand, the roof ridges of the temporary stands, the upper edges of the cars that had been left in the square — all gleamed softly in the starlight.

Very few people remained, and they were calling out their goodnights before heading off in their ones and twos.

From behind her came her sister's quiet, steady breathing. Now worn out and fast asleep, Jessica had spent the day walking — she'd been up and down every street in Notre-Dame-des-Bois,

190

she'd told Lauren — thinking through her options.

'But it's no use,' she'd said, heaving in a breath and letting it out on a long sigh. 'I just don't know what to do for the best.'

'Give it time. It's not the sort of thing you can decide all at once.'

'We're both in a pickle, aren't we?' Jessica had said with a wan smile, and Lauren had found it impossible to disagree.

She stared out across the dark square, her thoughts going back to the late afternoon. Jessica had insisted on going down to watch as the cars came back from their jaunt round the neighbouring villages, and Lauren's eyes had been drawn — inevitably — to Rafe.

When he went with Patrick and Bob to lock the cars in the garage for the night, she'd watched his tall, broad-shouldered frame until he disappeared from view, and it was a bittersweet pain to be — still — so aware of him.

Respite had come with the evening

meal. Friends of his had come down from Tours and they all sat at one end of one of the long lines of trestle tables while Lauren and the UK contingent were at the other end.

A fact that hadn't gone unnoticed by the deputy mayor. They'd seen him work his way down the tables, glad-handing almost every person there.

'Must be an election coming up some time soon,' Patrick had commented.

'Tsk tsk,' the man had said when he reached them. He shook his head. 'You British. So insular. Even young Raphaël abandons you.'

The lights in the Café des Sports went off and the square was in darkness. Movement beside the bandstand caught her eye, a darker shadow in the shadows. The fox again. Or a cat.

No. Lauren frowned. Too big, too tall. It was a man. And there was something stealthy about the way he moved. Her heart skidded into a faster beat.

Why had the man waited until the café lights went off? What was he doing out there in the darkness?

    She could think of only one answer.

No Going Back

Lauren didn't think twice. Swinging away from the window she crossed to the wardrobe, pulled out a black T-shirt and swiftly swapped it for the light green one she'd been wearing. Her jeans were dark, as were her trainers. Twisting her hair into a knot at the back of her head and fastening it with a comb, she stuffed the B&B keys into the back pocket of her jeans and let herself out of the room.

At the top of the stairs she hesitated. Should she wake Rafe? But that would take time, time she couldn't afford. Best not.

She ran down the stairs and out of the front door, closing it quietly behind her, and paused, pulses racing, needing a moment or two to get her bearings.

The sky was black velvet, pierced by countless millions of stars, tiny pin-points of light far brighter and far closer than they ever were back home. Little by little, her eyes adjusted, making the most of the meagre light, and she could make out the paler shadows of a wall or the side of a stall.

Moving at speed, she headed for the bandstand, zigzagging between stalls and cars and trees. Her trainers were soft-soled and made no noise. She slowed as she drew near. Was the man still there? Had he simply moved round to the other side? Was he hiding in the space beneath the raised structure?

How she wished she had a torch. Her heart was thumping, beating a wild tattoo against her ribcage.

Slowly, keeping her distance, she circled the bandstand. No-one. Drawing closer, she circled again, running her fingers along the struts and poles that held it all in place. No way could anyone get through and hide beneath it.

Pausing, she took several long, slow breaths. She knew where she had to go next. If the man was the saboteur — and who else could it be skulking around at dead of night? — then he'd make for where the cars were. The lock-up garage.

Moments later, panting, she pulled to a halt on the edge of the square. The garage lay before her, on the other side of the road, and she took the time to look the building over.

The large sliding door was, thankfully, still closed. The windows were dark shadows, but on the first floor above the entrance. Surely no-one could be hiding up there?

She looked to either side of the garage, at the hairdresser's on her left and the church on her right. Shadows, lots of them — and she felt sweat prick out on her palms.

An owl hooted, piercing the silence, making her start. She pulled the B&B keys from her pocket, holding them tight inside her fist in such a way that one key stuck out between her index and middle fingers. It was a weapon of sorts. Not much, but it might be enough.

She crossed the road running, tried the garage door. It wouldn't budge, was still firmly locked. Good. What to do next? Something — a sound? Movement? — made her twist round, and her foot caught against a stone, sending it skittering across the pavement.

It clattered, ringing, through the silence of the night, as loud as an explosion. Another small sound, this time from the direction of the church. An echo? Lauren didn't think so.

No. She'd found him. The saboteur. Hiding in the church porch.

She didn't stop to think. If she was right, this was the man who'd deliberately put three cars out of action, who'd caused unhappiness and heartbreak to herself and Jessica. To the others, too. Her shoulders went back, determination to confront the man driving her forward.

Again, an impression of something — movement? From behind her this time. She shivered, unnerved, and glanced back. Nothing.

She crossed to the church. Eyes fixed on the doorway, she started climbing the wide, shallow steps that led up to it. Yes, a man stood there, a darker shadow in the shadows. She couldn't see his face.

He had his arm across it, that was why, she saw, almost level with him. Two metres more and she'd have him.

A shout came from behind her.

And, in front, with a noise part growl, part sob, the man she'd been following burst out of the church porch, was running towards her, crashing into her, elbow of the arm that hid his face swinging round, thumping into her chin.

Her hand — the hand that gripped the keys — came up, met resistance, earned a grunted 'ouf' from her assailant. But it wasn't enough, and she was going down, down on to the hard stone steps.

★   ★   ★

'Lau-ren. Lauren, *ma chère*. Say you're OK.'

Rafe's voice, low and urgent. The voice she'd heard moments before. Rafe's hand, fingertips moving as he smoothed her hair back from her face. For a long, bewildered instant she didn't understand. Rafe was her with her? How was it possible?

It was dark. She could make out the shape of his head, see the gleam in his eyes, but little else. She lay on her back on ground that was cold, hard and uncomfortable.

She felt around beneath the arch of her spine: stone, and an unyielding right-angled edge. A step, she realised — and the events of the night came rushing back to her.

She was on one of the steps that led up to the church and she'd been face to face with the saboteur.

'I almost —' She stopped. Her voice wasn't right. She sounded dazed.

'Lauren, thank goodness. No, stay still.' His hand moved to her shoulder, restraining her. 'I'm calling an ambulance.'

She lifted her head a fraction, saw he was holding a phone to his ear.

'No need.' But it came out as a groan, and she sank back on to the step.

'I should never have let it happen,' he said, and she could hear the bitter self-reproach in his voice. 'I should have called out to you, got to him before you, not put your life at risk. What on earth were you doing here, at this time of night?'

'I saw him, by the bandstand. He was acting —' She searched for the word. 'Furtively, and I knew he was the saboteur. I knew I had to stop him.'

'Oh Lauren.' He broke off to speak at length in French. 'The ambulance crew will be here soon,' he said.

'I don't understand,' Lauren said. 'Were you following me?'

She sensed rather than saw him shake his head.

'Bob and I have been here since eleven.'

'Bob's here, too?'

'He was inside the lock-up, keeping an eye on the cars. I was over by the hairdresser's.'

'Oh.' It was an effort to make sense of it all.

'Patrick and Dave are going to take over at three.'

'Patrick and Dave?' Lauren found

herself repeating. That feeling of bewilderment was back, hadn't gone away in fact. She was having difficulty taking everything in. 'Where's Bob now?'

She shifted on to her side, propping herself up on her elbow, and looked towards the garage although it was too dark to make out anything more than the pale expanse of a wall. Her fingers met something metallic, something that jangled.

'My keys.' She curled her hand round them. 'I was holding them. I think I got him. He might be hurt.'

She braced herself, poised to push herself up into a sitting position.

'Stay where you are.' Both Rafe's hands were at her shoulders, gently but firmly pushing her back down. 'You might have broken something.' He swore under his breath. 'Why doesn't that ambulance get here?'

'It's my chin that hurts. He walloped me with his elbow.' But she wiggled her fingers and toes, testing for pain, just in case, and let out a sigh of relief.

Everything appeared to be working properly. Her brain, too, seemed to have cleared.

'So who planned this surveillance operation?' she asked, frowning as she thought things through, and felt his hands tighten their grip round her shoulders.

'You?'

There was the briefest of hesitations, as if he knew — and didn't relish — where her question would lead.

'Yes.'

'Yet you didn't think of telling me about it.' Even as she spoke, she realised why, and hot colour washed up into her face. Her bruised jawbone throbbed.

'Because of Jessica. You still weren't sure about her. But now you know! She's not the one who thumped into me, pushed me over.'

Another brief hesitation, and Lauren wished she could see his face.

'You're right. I do know now,' he said quietly, 'and I deeply regret the hurt I've caused her — and you.'

It was a courteous apology, and clearly sincere, and Lauren welcomed it. Even so, she couldn't simply forget the bitterness, the anger, his suspicions concerning her sister had provoked. The memory of it all was bound to linger. For a while at least.

A silence stretched between them, broken only by the sound of approaching footsteps. It was Bob, together with Belle. The Labrador whined as though sensing the tension that crackled around her, and pushed herself in between Lauren and Rafe.

'The ambulance can't be much longer,' Rafe muttered. 'I phoned ages ago.'

'How are you feeling, Lauren, love?' Bob crouched down next to the other man. 'A bit better than you were ten minutes ago, I bet.' He spoke in the jaunty sing-song of someone putting on a show of cheerfulness.

'I thought I'd bring Belle back with me,' he went on, part-turning to Rafe. 'She's not trained to follow scents or anything but, well, you never know.'

'A long shot, but worth trying,' Rafe murmured. 'Ah. The ambulance. Thank goodness for that.'

He scrambled to his feet, his relief evident, and in no time at all Lauren was strapped on to a stretcher, ready to be placed inside the vehicle.

'They tell me I've got to sit in the front,' he said.

'You're coming with me?' Lauren's heart leaped but her voice, she hoped, gave nothing away. She could, at last, see Rafe's face in the ambulance headlights. His expression, though, was unreadable.

'Bob'll stay here. I don't think the guy will come back. But if he does, we're prepared. And you might need someone to translate for you.'

Did his expression soften as he touched his finger to her cheek? Or did she simply imagine it?

★ ★ ★

'So, how's the invalid this morning?' In a floral print dress, all pinks and reds and oranges, her sister was a burst of bright energy as she swept into the hospital room.

'I'm not an invalid,' Lauren said, wincing as she pushed herself up into a sitting position.

'No need to get all grumpy.' Jessica let the bags she was carrying drop on to the bed.

'I'm not —' Lauren laughed. 'Or maybe I am. It was a long night.'

'I've brought you a change of clothes. And your toothbrush, of course. The taxi'll be here at half past.' Jessica sat down on the edge of the bed, taking one of Lauren's hands in both hers.

Her eyes narrowed as she scanned the lower half of her sister's face.

'You've got a bit of a bruise on your chin. Any bumps anywhere else?'

'Not really. A few here and there from when I fell down the church steps. They'll soon go.'

'No broken bones, thank goodness.'

'No.' She'd been examined and x-rayed, and given a clean bill of health. She'd be leaving the hospital as soon as she'd showered and dressed.

'You had quite a night of it, I gather. Bob and Rafe have been telling us all about it. We all got together for an early coffee,' Jessica explained.

Rafe. A smile curved Lauren's lips. He'd stayed with her for hours while she underwent the various tests and hadn't left until gone three in the morning.

'Though it was worse than pulling teeth,' Jessica was saying. 'We were having to positively prise the information out of Rafe.'

The words brought Lauren out of her reverie.

'Rafe?' she said. 'I don't know the whole story, either.'

'We-ell. Are you sitting comfortably? Shall I fluff up your pillows?'

'Just get on with it,' Lauren said with a laugh. 'I know where they both were. Tell me what they saw and did.'

'OK.' Jessica grew serious. 'Well. A

man — a dark figure — appeared. On the edge of the square, between two trees. He stood there for a while. Listening? Watching? Waiting?

'Rafe didn't know, but he messaged Bob inside the lock-up, alerting him. Then the figure ran across to the church, up the steps and into the doorway.'

Lauren shivered, her sister's words stirring unwelcome memories.

'Go on,' she said.

'Seconds later, you appeared. In exactly the same spot. Only Rafe didn't know it was you, of course. His first thought was there were two of you, working together. Accomplices.

'When you went over to the garage and tried the door, that confirmed it in his mind. Bob was the other side of it, by the way, brandishing a tyre lever,' she added.

'Oh!' The word came out as a gasp.

'Keeping his distance, Rafe was following you as you headed towards the church.'

'Ah.' Yes, she'd glanced behind her

with that uneasy feeling someone was there.

'He called out a — he says — reasonably polite something. And suddenly everything changed. You were sprawled over the steps and the other guy was running away.

'Remember, he still had it in mind the two of you were working together. You weren't moving — he could safely leave it to Bob to make sure you didn't get away — and he ran off after the other guy.'

And all at once Lauren understood.

'That's what he was beating himself up about,' she said, as much to herself as to her sister.

'He lost the other guy in the maze of cars and trees and stuff, and came back to find it was you he'd left to Bob's tender mercies. He was devastated.' Jessica paused. 'He loves you, Lauren,' she added.

And she rather feared she still loved him.

The Chase Is On

The church bells were ringing when the taxi deposited Lauren and her sister outside their B&B, reminding her it was Sunday and the last day of the rally. A feeling of sadness swept over her.

Tomorrow morning, the others would be setting off, making the return trip to the ferry and on to the UK. Not her and Jessica, though. Nor Sarah and Dave. They'd have to wait until their petrol tanks had been cleaned out and their cars were fit to run. They wouldn't be travelling till Tuesday at the earliest.

And what of Rafe? He'd surely be leaving tomorrow, keen to continue to repair the damage his cousin Steve's sudden departure had done to the family business. She'd probably never see him again. Or rarely. At another classic car rally perhaps.

All at once her throat was tight, and she swallowed against the unexpected pain of it. She'd told him she didn't want to see him any more. That it was over between them.

So why did she have to keep reminding herself of the fact? And why did it hurt so much?

'Hey, come on.' Jessica caught Lauren's fingers in hers. 'You're looking a bit down. Let me pop these things upstairs, and we'll go and find the others.'

They found them — inevitably — on the terrace of the Café des Sports. Inevitable too was the way everyone stood up to give the new arrivals 'good morning' kisses. A French custom the whole group had adopted with great enthusiasm, Lauren thought, smiling, her normal good humour coming back a little.

Still smiling when she reached Rafe, she felt her expression falter a fraction. He faced her, standing close, and she inhaled the familiar scent of him. He was studying her features, his gaze as soft as a caress, and her breath caught.

She stood on tiptoes to give him a kiss on each cheek, her lips far too aware of the delicious rasp of his skin against them. How she wished he'd wrap her in his arms, gathering her to him as he'd done not so long ago.

'It's good to see you out of hospital,' he said.

'It's good to be out.' Only she, Lauren hoped, could detect the slight tremble in her voice.

'Have the bruises calmed down a bit?' His hand started to come up, and she flinched, thinking he was going to touch the bruise on her chin. His eyes narrowed, hand dropping back to his side.

'A bit,' she said. 'How did you get back to the B&B? No taxis at three in the morning, I bet.'

'I jogged. It's not far. A couple of kilometres.'

'Good.' Lauren was appalled at herself. Was she really having this stilted exchange with him? Was this the best she could do? Squaring her shoulders, she drew in a steadying breath.

'The doctors and nurses were lovely, but I — I must thank you for being there with me. I really appreciated it.'

'You know I'd —' He stopped abruptly and gave a light, easy smile instead. 'If you need anything, just ask.'

Whatever he was going to say, he'd clearly changed his mind, and Lauren was inexplicably saddened.

As usual, they pushed three of the café's outside tables together to make one long thin one. Seeing Rafe go down one side, Lauren went down the other. That way, she reasoned, she wouldn't have to endure the exquisite torture of sitting next to him.

To her dismay, she found herself sitting opposite him and that was possibly worse because it was an effort to tear her eyes away from him.

'OK, ladies and gentlemen.' Patrick, sitting at one end, rapped the side of his phone twice against the metal table.

'Calling the meeting to order,' Rafe murmured, and Lauren couldn't help smiling, though she kept her eyes fixed on Patrick.

'We need to go over the events of last night,' her ex continued, 'and decide what we're going to do, how we're going to approach things, today.'

'Last night — well!' Jessica, sitting on Lauren's right, addressed the group as a whole. Her voice, saccharine sweet, had a brittle edge to it. 'Patrick, Dave, Bob and Rafe playing vigilantes — who'd have believed it?'

Lauren heard a couple of swift intakes of breath. Belle, stretched out on the pavement behind Brenda, lifted her head and whined.

'It wasn't a game, Jess,' she said quietly.

'Nice to be invited to this morning's get-together,' Jessica went on. She turned to her sister. 'No prizes for guessing why you and I weren't even told about last night's little party.'

It was spoken lightly but Lauren could hear the bitterness that lingered close to the surface.

'I bet Brenda and Sarah and Chrissie knew about it.'

Everyone looked uncomfortable, and it crossed Lauren's mind that Rafe wasn't the only one who'd suspected her sister of sabotage.

Colour stained his cheeks. He looked down at his hands, clasped together on the table, then across at Jessica.

'It was my fault, Jessica. My fault entirely. The others followed my lead. I said you — and your sister —' His gaze moved to Lauren, and she could see the anguish that shadowed his eyes and tightened his jaw.

'I said you should be kept out of the loop. I got it wrong, and I apologise. Unreservedly. I know now you've had nothing whatsoever to do with what's been going on.

'I seem to make a habit of getting things wrong,' he added, more to himself than to any of the others.

There was no doubting his sincerity. For a long moment Jessica met his gaze and said nothing. Then the tension eased from her shoulders, and her features softened into a smile.

'Apology accepted, Rafe. Thank you for it.'

Relief all round, and a burst of conversation. The waiter came to take their orders. Lauren mouthed a heartfelt 'Thank you' across the table to Rafe before tearing her eyes away.

She couldn't bear to look at him. She still loved him. What a fool she'd been. Sucking in a deep breath, she turned to Bob who sat at the opposite end of the three tables to Patrick and brought a smile to her face.

'How did sniffer dog Belle get on last night?'

Bob smiled back.

'Well, she had a good sniff round where the guy had been lurking — but didn't go chasing after anyone's scent, I'm afraid.'

'More's the pity,' Dave said.

The café owner hadn't yet pulled the awning out, and the sun was warm on her face and arms. The waiter was going round the table setting their orders, complete with biscuit and sugar cubes, in front of each of them, filling the still air with the enticing aroma of coffee.

She turned and looked behind her, over the road to the square. Most of the cars, she thought, were already in place, and people were walking around in twos or threes or small groups admiring the vehicles, chatting with their owners, or stopping to buy something from one of the stalls.

From time to time there was a flash as the sun caught the brass instruments being unpacked on the bandstand. The oompah band, Lauren thought, smiling. The square wouldn't remain quiet for much longer.

Patrick rapped twice on the table with his phone and she turned back round to face the others — and Rafe.

'We now know,' Patrick said, 'that there is a saboteur —'

'We owe apologies to Rafe,' Bob chipped in, 'for doubting him on that score.' There were murmurs of agreement.

'Yes, of course,' Patrick said stiffly.

'This is turning into a morning for apologies, it seems. But thank you.' Rafe dipped his head in acknowledgement. 'Apology accepted.'

'We also know it's not one of us.'

'Yes, valid point, Sarah. So who is this guy?'

'And why's he doing it?' Lauren added.

'What's his motive?'

'I suggest,' Rafe said, 'that we look first at arrangements for today and how we can keep the cars safe. They're in the lock-up garage at the moment.

'They can stay there until after lunch when we'll all go along — in our costumes — and get them out for this afternoon's grand parade. We'll each stay with our own car till after the final judging, and put them back in the garage before the farewell dinner and dance this evening. How does that sound? Are we all agreed?'

There were no dissenting voices, and Lauren smiled to herself. How effortlessly Rafe had taken charge of the meeting.

'Could this guy have got into the

lock-up last night?'

'Good question, Chrissie.'

'I don't think he had any tools with him,' Lauren said. 'So why did he go there? What was he hoping to do?'

'Checking the place out?'

'Maybe we ought to post a permanent guard, even —'

'Agreed, whenever the cars are there, not just at night.'

Only half-listening, Lauren twisted round and looked out over the square. It was filling up with people of all ages out to enjoy the cars, the various stalls, and the warmth of the day. The noise level was rising, laughter, excited chat, and squeaky practice notes from the oom-pah band echoing from the buildings all around.

Lauren breathed out on a long sigh. Three acts of sabotage, her car, Rafe's and Dave and Sarah's Austin. Three acts of sabotage that had to be connected in some way. Yet they seemed so random. Something linked the three. But what?

She saw the deputy mayor holding

court over at the buvette, the wine-by-the-glass stall. He smiled and raised his glass to her.

Here was someone who never had a good word to say about the British. Was he the saboteur? But that was rubbish. Lauren dismissed the notion immediately. For a start, one of their number was French, not British.

From the bandstand came a breathy blast of sound as a trumpeter tried his instrument out. And there was Aurélien, in mid-stride as he walked past the raised structure, already in costume for the afternoon, unmistakable in his fedora and dove-grey 1920s suit with its bright amber stripe. He saw her, and she lifted her hand, about to beckon him over, invite him to have a coffee with them.

Checking his stride the merest fraction, he turned his head away. Something jerky — furtive, almost — about the way he did it lifted the hairs at Lauren's nape. All at once, she was seized by the conviction it was an accident their eyes had met — an accident he hadn't wanted to happen.

And that could only mean one thing.

No time to think. Even as she turned, eyes going to Rafe — an automatic reaction — she was scraping her chair back, springing to her feet.

'Aurélien, wait!'

She crossed the road at a run, dodging round people, side-stepping buggies, trying to keep the fedora and dove-grey suit in view.

She darted a glance behind her. Rafe was up, moving swiftly along the line of tables past Chrissie and Patrick. The others too were getting to their feet, quickly, despite the puzzlement on their faces.

She'd lost him. No, there he was, some 20 metres ahead of her, walking still but moving fast. He'd gone round the bandstand, was heading back in the direction he'd come from.

'Aurélien,' she called. 'Stop.'

Fifteen metres. She was catching up. But the throng was denser now, and she was having to slow her pace. Biting her lip in frustration, she struggled to get past people who stood or strolled, stopped walking or changed direction without warning.

'Lauren. Where are you?' A shout, from Rafe, from somewhere behind her. She looked back, couldn't see him through the mass of people. But she couldn't stop. She had to go on.

Aurélien had turned to his right, was making his way along a line of agricultural vehicles. There were fewer people here. He looked behind him. His eyes caught Lauren's. Pulling his hat off, he broke into a run.

'Aurélien!' Lauren too was running. But her heart was pumping an uneasy beat. Was she doing the right thing? Or was she being incredibly foolish? Aurélien, really? Was he the saboteur? The person she'd had friendly conversations with? He'd deliberately damaged three valuable cars? It was almost impossible to reconcile the two.

The Frenchman suddenly jolted to a halt. Swivelling on his heels he turned to face her, and her stomach swooped.

His chest rose and fell. He certainly didn't look his usual well-groomed self, Lauren thought, taking in the plaster on the side of his jaw and the speck of blood below it on the collar of his shirt.

She hesitated, but only for a moment. She'd had to chase after him and that gave her confidence.

'It's you, isn't it? You're the one who's been sabotaging our cars.'

Aurélien pushed his hat back on his head and straightened his tie. He stood some two metres away, facing her.

'I? Sabotaging your cars? That is ridiculous.'

'I don't know how — or when exactly — but you somehow managed to go down to the car decks during the ferry crossing, and you turned the radiator drain tap on the Bentley.'

'Nonsense. You are delusional, Lauren.' He glanced round and up at the combine harvester on his left and the tractors behind him, and took a small step backwards.

'I left my car out in the square the first night we were here. You could have come along at any time to pour water into the petrol tank.'

''Could' but did not. All this is pure conjecture.'

'And yesterday —' Was it only yesterday? So much had happened since then. She chanced a look behind her. Where was Rafe? Where were the others? The agricultural vehicles were massive — the wheels alone were as tall as a man — and enclosed the two of them on three sides. Would Rafe, or anyone, ever find her? 'Yesterday you were in the café with us. You could have —'

''Could' again, Lauren.' He shook his head and spoke slowly, sadly, as if imparting an unwelcome truth. 'As I tell my pupils, 'could' expresses a possibility, not a certainty. You are speculating, mademoiselle. You have no proof.' The glimmer of a smile curved his mouth. 'You can't prove a thing against me.'

A different note had entered his voice. Triumph. Lauren's heart jumped a beat. He thought he'd won, that he was invulnerable. And that was a mistake — she'd been right.

Her chin came up and she gestured towards the plaster on his jaw.

'I thought at first you'd cut yourself shaving. But you didn't, did you? I did that to you. Last night.'

His smile vanished. Lauren's steady gaze met his. Long seconds stretched. For the first time he looked uncertain.

Then his shoulders sagged and he looked away, to one side, to the other, as if no longer able to meet her eyes.

'All right. Yes,' he said at last. 'I did it. It was me.'

A Dream Come True

Aurélien's lip curled.

'You know why?'

'I think I can guess. Your wife —'

'My ex-wife. Thanks to her and her grasping, selfish ways —' He broke off, heaving in a sharp breath. 'I used to love the UK, used to love all things British. It is why I spent so much time there, why I loved the language and became an English teacher. It is how I met and married her.' He spat the word out.

'Go on.' Something close to sorrow softened Lauren's voice. What he'd done was wrong. At the same time, though, she could feel — and understand — his pain.

'I couldn't bear the thought of another lot of Brits — you and your friends — getting the better of me. Winning the best of show prize. For the third year running.

'What a kick in the teeth that would have been. I had to stop it happening. I had to stop you.' He fell silent just as the oompah band launched into a lively rendition of 'Yankee Doodle Dandy'. From nearby came shouts.

'She's here!'

'They're both here.' Rafe burst out from between the combine harvester and one of the tractors. In an instant, he'd crossed the gap between them, gathering her into his arms, crushing her to him.

'Lauren, *mon coeur*. You're safe now. Did he hurt you?'

'Oh, Rafe.' Her heart was singing yet she wanted to cry. The sheer joy of seeing him, of being in his arms again, sent a wave of emotion surging through her. 'No. No, he didn't.'

Bob and Dave had been close behind. Before Aurélien could even think of moving, they each took hold of one of his arms.

'There is no need for that.' Angrily, the Frenchman shrugged their hands away. 'I will not run off.'

Rafe's arms were holding her tight. He was murmuring soft words, pressing kisses to her hair. It was an effort to lift her head.

She looked at Aurélien. Holding his hat in both hands, he stood straight and tall, and she had the impression of a man calmly resigned to hearing his fate.

Perhaps telling his story, getting his bitterness out into the open, had been cathartic for him.

'He confessed. But —' She hesitated. What would happen if they went to the gendarmes and he was prosecuted and found guilty, as he surely would be? Would he lose his teaching job? Would he be fined — or jailed? Did what he'd done really warrant that?

'I don't think we should report him to the gendarmes.'

She sensed rather than heard his exhalation of relief, drowned out as it was by the music from the oompah band.

'I suppose it's our word against his,' Bob said. 'We can't prove —'

'That's all very well,' Dave protested, 'but he's damaged my car. Is he going to pay for it?'

'Round up the others,' Rafe cut in. 'All go back to the café — Aurélien included — and decide what you should do for the best.'

'What about you two?'

Her breath caught in her throat as Rafe's thumb traced the line of her jaw where the bruise was.

'We'll join you later,' he said.

Aurélien put his hat back on his head.

'Thank you,' he said quietly, tipping the fedora's brim to Lauren. Flanked by Bob and Dave, he set off in the direction of the café.

For a moment, neither she nor Rafe moved. Neither spoke. Then he drew her against him.

'Are you sure you're all right?' he asked.

'You were trembling.'

'Relief — you'd found me.' She couldn't help shuddering.

'Oh, Lauren.' His voice was husky with emotion. 'If anything had happened to you, I'd never have forgiven myself.' His arms tightened their hold as though he'd never let her go.

'He wouldn't have hurt me.' Lauren's head was pressed against his chest, and her words were muffled. 'He's not a violent man. I'm pretty sure of that.'

Rafe stroked her hair, pressed kisses to the top of her head. Lauren was trembling still, warm and safe in his arms but conscious too of the dangerous thrill of excitement his embrace always provoked.

'Lauren.' Something about the way he spoke her name made her lift her head from his chest. 'These last twenty-four hours have been the worst kind of torture.

'There you were, so close — but untouchable. I wanted to hold you, talk and laugh with you — but you'd put a fence around yourself.'

'I was angry with you,' she murmured.

'You were right to be angry with me. I somehow had it fixed in my mind that Jessica was responsible for the sabotage. I couldn't think beyond that.'

'Rafe — even I had my doubts about

her.'

Lauren saw pain in his eyes as he smoothed strands of her hair back from her face. He shook his head.

'You said there were some things we have to take on trust and again you were right. I should have taken on trust that you know your sister much better than I do.

'If only we could put it behind us. If only I —' He stopped, his gaze moving from her hair to her eyes to her mouth. 'I love you, Lauren. Say you love me too.'

Her heart stood still, then soared.

'Yes.' The word was no more than a breath. 'Yes, I do.'

★   ★   ★

'You look gorgeous,' Jessica said.

It was early evening and she was fastening the line of tiny fabric-covered buttons that ran down the back of the dress her sister was going to wear for the farewell dinner and dance.

In a fine sapphire blue crepe, long and

bias-cut, it hugged Lauren's curves in a way that made her feel wonderfully feminine. She twisted to one side so that she could examine her back view in the mirror.

'There are fifty of them,' Jessica said. 'Fifty buttons. The two of you have made up, I take it.

'It's written all over your face.'

'He told me he loved me,' Lauren said, voice soft with the wonder of it.

The rest of the day, all of it spent with Rafe, had taken on a dream-like quality. They'd walked and talked, hand in hand through the town, or he'd swung her round, pulling her against him, his hands clasping her face as he kissed her.

They wouldn't take part in the grand parade, they decided — their time together was too precious. It was almost as if they had to make up for the lost hours.

By common accord they'd made their way to the woods on the edge of town, following the path till they came to the river. It was warm, the air was still, and they found a spot close-by where dappled light and shade played over them and the only sounds were the rippling of the water over stones and the sweet songs of birds.

'I'm so glad.' Jessica's voice broke into her memories.

Lauren laughed.

'You've changed your tune.' There was no sharpness in the remark. She was beyond happy, couldn't be cross with anyone, not even her sister.

'Well, Steve says Rafe —'

'Steve?'

'Yes. We're back in contact.' Jessica beamed a smile, and it struck Lauren that, yes, there was now a bounce in Jessica's movements and a ready smile on her face.

'That's brilliant news, Jess.'

'I messaged him. I've had a rethink about the whole settling down and starting a family thing. I've realised it's not an either-or issue. Either career or babies. And Steve needs to be involved.

'Anyway, we're talking about it again, that's the main thing.'

'I'm so pleased,' Lauren said, pulling her sister into a hug. 'So what does Steve say about his cousin?'

'He's got nothing but praise for him. A great guy, he says.'

Lauren's smile broadened.

'I know. I agree,' she said simply.

There was a knock at the door. Rafe, looking magnificent in a double-breasted dinner jacket and wide-legged trousers. He smiled when he saw her and all at once she was breathless.

'Nineteen-thirties clothes suit you,' she said, standing on tiptoes to kiss him.

'You look lovely,' he murmured, and there was infinite tenderness in the way he was looking at her.

'You two go on ahead,' Jessica called from inside the room. 'I need to touch up my make-up.'

Rafe's eyes gleamed.

'Tactfully leaving the lovebugs together?'

Lauren laughed.

'I rather think you're right.'

'Then shall we go?' he said, hooking

his arm round hers.

As before, that evening's meal would be served at long rows of trestle tables, set up outside the salle des fêtes. A space at one end had been boarded over for the dancing after the meal.

They found the others standing in a group in the middle of one of the rows.

'We've baggsed places for everyone,' Sarah said.

'Where did you two get to?' Dave asked.

'We had to decide what to do about Aurélien,' Patrick said, a hint of petulance in his voice. 'You should have been here.'

Chrissie wasn't standing next to him, Lauren saw. Maybe that explained his bad mood.

'We had some talking to do,' Rafe said in a tone that ended that particular conversation.

'Do a twirl, Lauren, love. Another of Jessica's creations? You look fantastic.'

Rafe caught her fingers in his.

'She always does.'

'So what did you decide?' Lauren asked just as her sister, looking radiant in a long black dress threaded with silver, joined them.

'Not to report him to the gendarmes,' Bob said.

'Good,' she breathed.

'But he's going to pay all the garage bills. And he pulled out of the grand parade this afternoon. We thought it would be inappropriate if he were to win the best of show prize.'

'That Lancia of his is immaculate,' Sarah put in, 'and he's always dressed impeccably, so there was a real chance he might.'

'Where is he now?' Rafe asked. 'Is he here?'

Bob shook his head.

'No. He's gone home.'

'And did he explain how or when he managed to get down to the car decks during the ferry crossing?' Lauren asked. Rafe stood close at her side, his arm round her waist, and it was an effort to think about anything else.

'Yes. Easy-peasy. Right at the beginning of the trip,' Dave said. 'We all went upstairs but he doubled back. If any of us had noticed him going back down to the car decks — not that any of us did — he'd simply have said he'd forgotten something.'

'What about last night? What was he hoping to do?'

'He says it had become an obsession, putting the British entries out of the running. He went there, yes, but with no particular plan in mind. He didn't even have a key.'

'Oh, and Belle kept growling and circling round him,' Brenda added. 'I reckon she had picked up his scent last night.'

There was good-natured laughter as Lauren and Rafe stooped to stroke the Labrador and murmur 'Good dog', and everyone took their places on the bench seats either side of the trestle table.

A good while later, and Lauren sighed a happy sigh. The food had doubtless been delicious, but she had little recollection of what she'd eaten. Her thoughts were all of Rafe, her senses revelling in his warmth and closeness.

Now that the meal was over, the rally organisers were due to announce the winner of the best of show prize.

The microphone squealed, conversations stopped as everyone paused to listen. The announcements were in French, of course, but Lauren recognised the name that came at the end.

'Philippe Lepage? Monsieur Lepage has won?' She twisted round to check with Rafe. He nodded, and she settled back against him.

'I'm glad it's someone we know,' she murmured. It somehow made her happiness even more perfect.

The band launched into an early-sixties medley, and soon Brenda and Bob were on the dance floor, her pony tail swinging, his quiff flopping as they threw themselves into a jive. Sarah and Dave were with them, laughing as they tried to copy the moves.

Patrick and Chrissie were there, too. But something about the set of Chrissie's mouth reminded Lauren how it had been for herself with Patrick and she sensed — with a tinge of sadness in her heart because she wanted everyone to be as happy as she was — that the relationship wasn't going to last.

Her sister had moved further along the bench. Belle was at her feet, chin resting on front paws, one eye open. Jessica had her phone in her hand and a smile on her face.

No prizes for guessing who she was contacting, Lauren thought with another happy sigh. How she hoped her sister and Steve would rediscover the happiness they'd once shared.

Rafe touched her wrist in a way that sent a shiver of excitement darting across her skin.

'Would you like to dance?'

Once again she twisted round to face him and a smile curved her lips as her hand moved to the nape of his neck, gently pulling him towards her.

'Maybe later,' she breathed.

We do hope that you have enjoyed reading this large print book.

Did you know that all of our titles are available for purchase?

We publish a wide range of high quality large print books including:
Romances, Mysteries, Classics
General Fiction
Non Fiction and Westerns

Special interest titles available in large print are:
The Little Oxford Dictionary
Music Book, Song Book
Hymn Book, Service Book

Also available from us courtesy of Oxford University Press:
Young Readers' Dictionary
(large print edition)
Young Readers' Thesaurus
(large print edition)

For further information or a free brochure, please contact us at:
Ulverscroft Large Print Books Ltd.,
The Green, Bradgate Road, Anstey,
Leicester, LE7 7FU, England.
Tel: (00 44) **0116 236 4325**
Fax: (00 44) **0116 234 0205**

Other titles in the
Linford Romance Library:

A STRANGER COMES

Ewan Smith

Velma is a lively young widow who runs a thriving inn in the bustling port of Evenmouth. Her reputation as a hostess is unrivalled, and even Lady Osanna and Lord Durwin at the castle often seek her help when putting on their banquets. Now, she watches with interest as a curious ship from distant parts comes in with the tide. She will soon find that there is something oddly familiar about the intriguing stranger who arrives with it . . .